I0627506

Books by
Sharon & James Brubaker

Meadowood Gardens Mysteries
HALF PAST DEATH

Books by
Sharon Brubaker

Selkie Sisters Series
BETWEEN EARTH & SEA
BETWEEN SEA & SAND
MEMORIES OF THE SEA (Novella)

Sea Glass Series
TIDES OF BLUE
CURRENTS OF BLUE

HALF PAST DEATH

BOOK ONE

SHARON BRUBAKER

JAMES BRUBAKER

*This book is dedicated in memory of our friend,
Sarah Detmer, for good conversations about
gardens and writing.*

ACKNOWLEDGMENTS

We are grateful to our loving and supportive friends and family. Thank you to Kris and Jon Barry and the Groff's Plant Farm staff, Kirkwood, PA, and Faith Redcay. Also, thanks to Meredith S. K. Boas of Grunge Muffin Designs and Sheila Reist. Special thanks to Alice Lundgren, Linda Roller, and Jodi Jackola for their friendship, support, beta-reading, and adventuring.

Thank you...
Meredith S. K. Boas, for the cover art.
Maria Alliaud, for the Meadowood Map.
Nova Jarvis, for your edits.
Dax, for being the perfect model for the character Nepeta.

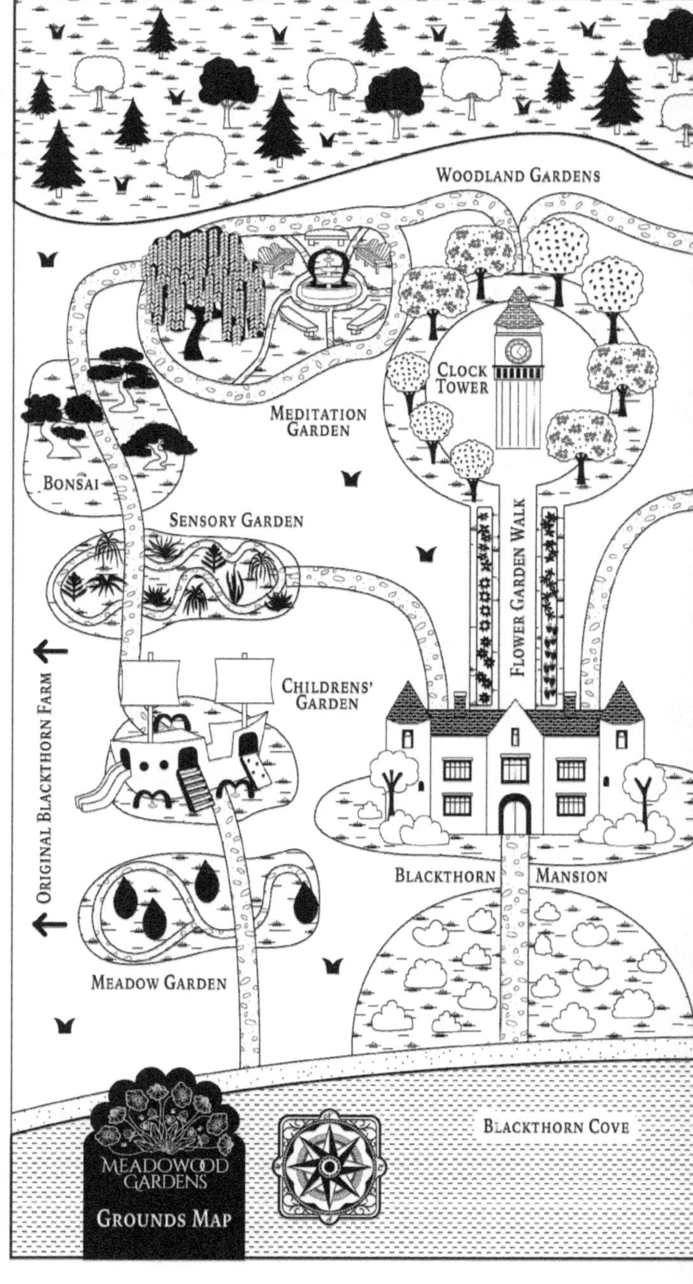

WOODLAND GARDENS
MEDITATION GARDEN
CLOCK TOWER
BONSAI
SENSORY GARDEN
ORIGINAL BLACKTHORN FARM
CHILDRENS' GARDEN
FLOWER GARDEN WALK
BLACKTHORN MANSION
MEADOW GARDEN
BLACKTHORN COVE
MEADOWOOD GARDENS
GROUNDS MAP

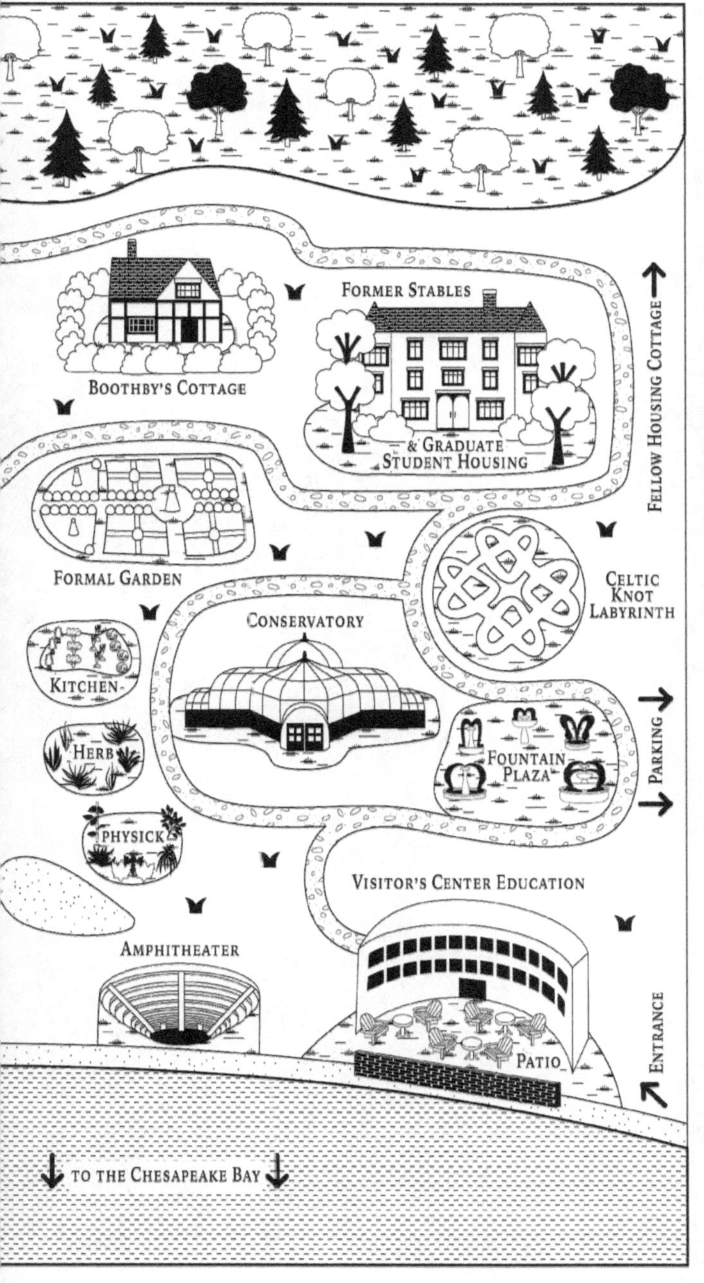

BOOTHBY'S COTTAGE
FORMER STABLES
& GRADUATE STUDENT HOUSING
FELLOW HOUSING COTTAGE
FORMAL GARDEN
CELTIC KNOT LABYRINTH
KITCHEN
CONSERVATORY
HERB
FOUNTAIN PLAZA
PARKING
PHYSICK
VISITOR'S CENTER EDUCATION
AMPHITHEATER
PATIO
ENTRANCE
TO THE CHESAPEAKE BAY

MEADOW
GARDEN

n.b. The pronunciation of Marigold Saille's surname is "Sal-yeh" in Irish. Marigold is of Scottish-Irish descent. Saille is Ogham term for 'willow.'

CHAPTER ONE

Marigold Saille woke to the early morning sun and a purring hulk of an orange tabby cat snuggled beside her like a teddy bear. As she opened her eyes, Nepeta stopped purring to bop her gently on the nose and give it a lick.

"Oh, you gorgeous cat, Nepeta," Mari crooned. "I need to get up and get ready!"

Mari squeezed her eyes shut in joy. She couldn't believe her luck. She was officially a student in the Master's program at Meadowood Botanic Gardens. As a young child, Mari often told her family that she would someday live at Meadowood—and here she was after applying for the graduate program in Public Garden Administration in her senior year of college.

Mari had always loved gardens. Observing plants, digging about, and reading everything she could about plants were her favorite pastimes. Growing up, *The Secret Garden* was one of her favorite books. She read her copy until it was in tatters. As a child, she insisted to her family that her jump rope was not a jump rope but a skipping rope, just like the character Mary Lennox in *The Secret Garden*. Mari remembered fussing about a wool coat as well. She wanted to look exactly like the illustrations in the book and threw a tantrum or two, hoping to get a coat that looked just like the character's. It was her grandmother who indulged her. She bought her the coat and placed a huge, old, brass key in the pocket. Mari pretended it was the key to the secret garden. And she still had the key. The key held a proud place on her desk, and the tattered copy of *The Secret Garden* was never far from her bedside.

Her siblings teased her and called her a 'plant-nerd' because she started saying the Latin names of the plants even as a kid. She liked the sound of the Latin and the way it rolled off her tongue. Mari agreed happily that she was a plant nerd and spoke in what she called "plant-speak," teasing them with unusual Latin names of plants and trees every chance she got.

Mari had been at Meadowood for nearly a week. She remembered the first day of orientation. She had personal interviews with the two horticulture professors. Dr. Fuller was an imposing woman. She had snappy dark eyes, and Mari knew she wouldn't take any excuse for late or shoddy work. She set the bar high on expectations. But, her office was neat and spare, filled with beautiful black and white photographs and paintings of trees and leaves. The walls were a calming shade of green. Mari was a little afraid of her but wanted to study under her, especially after learning that she had been at Meadowood for nearly fifteen years. Dr. Knight was the other horticulture professor. Mari felt a little nervous meeting him.

He was a notable professor in the field and a friend

of her grandfather's. Dr. Knight put her at ease immediately by offering her a 'spot of tea.' He used an electric kettle to boil water and poured it over loose tea leaves in a strainer over the teapot. Once brewed, he poured her a mug and offered her cream, sugar, and chocolate biscuits. It was like being at her grandparents' house. His snowy white hair, kind eyes, and gentle smile made her feel at home. She remembered her grandfather telling her about Dr. Knight's passion for King Arthur.

He had a replica of Excalibur hanging on the wall and a matching letter opener that peeked out from beneath piles of papers on his desk. His office had photographs of castles, heather, and the sea. Mari thought they were likely related to his passion for King Arthur. He even had a stained-glass window of Arthur pulling the sword from the stone in front of his window overlooking Meadowood. Dr. Knight and Mari shared stories of her grandfather, and soon, both were chuckling at reminiscences. Dr. Knight seemed very kind, almost like a British Mr. Rogers, but with steel underneath. She knew she would try her best to make him proud.

Mari had been visiting Meadowood Gardens once a month or more as she grew up. Nepeta, the large orange tabby cat snuggled in her arms, was her secret friend in the gardens. Nepeta was a garden cat Mari had met eight years ago while visiting with her family. She seemed to bump into him on every visit and started bringing treats along on any ensuing visits. He seemed to have a sixth sense about when she would arrive. Even her family noticed, teasing her that she would steal the cat from Meadowood someday. When she arrived for the Master's program, Nepeta was here to greet her. Even though pets weren't permitted in the graduate housing, everyone looked the other way.

Burying her face into the cat's soft fur caused Nepeta to purr loudly. She looked out the turret window over the gardens. In the distance, the sliver of silvery blue of the Chesapeake Bay was a brilliant backdrop to the beauty of Meadowood. Her window gave her a view of the Celtic Knot labyrinth below. She was fortunate to have won the lottery to get one of the turret rooms that looked out over the gardens rather than a view of the scrub of woods and parking lot for visitors. She had spent many hours tracing the intricate brick paths of the labyrinth with a tiptoe race on the bricks with her brother and sister. She had so many delightful memories of visiting the gardens with her family. Now she was here, entering a new, exciting chapter of her life. She squeezed Nepeta tightly in delight, and the cat gave an annoyed meow before scrambling out of her arms.

"Sorry, Nepeta," Mari apologized.

Glancing at the time, she yelped. She was late and hurried to dress in her khaki pants and a denim shirt with the Meadowood Gardens logo emblazoned on the upper left, the students' official uniform. When finished, she went downstairs to the community kitchen with Nepeta trailing behind.

The dormitory was three stories tall, had two turrets, and housed eight lucky graduate students working in the gardens and taking classes for a Master's program in Public Gardens Administration. When interviewed, the admissions director joked that she would learn everything from the ground up as a student at the gardens. Mari remembered the admissions counselor saying *Basically, you're an indentured servant to Meadowood Gardens during your tenure as a student. You will eat, sleep, breathe, and learn every facet of public garden administration.* Mari would happily be their indentured servant for a couple of years and could practice what she learned in her bachelor's degree in botany and horticulture. And here she was, now living twenty-four/seven, on the grounds in the dorms that used to be the old stables.

The eight graduate students in the Master's program were a somewhat elite lot. They lived in the renovated stables on the Meadowood grounds. The Common area consisted of a kitchen and living room on the main floor of the stables. The stable doors were replaced by large windows, which drenched the common area with sunshine. The inside walls were a creamy vellum color that reflected the sun. Someone had decorated the walls with gorgeous oversized photographs of plants. The shared area had a large television, comfy couches and chairs, and a kitchen.

Mari wrinkled her nose at the smell of bacon cooking. There, at the stove, was Joe Henry. He was tall, with black hair and blazing blue eyes. He lorded over the bacon and eggs cooking on the stove, wielding the spatula expertly.

"Good morning," he greeted Mari, teasing, knowing she was vegetarian. "Care for some bacon and eggs?"

Mari's stomach churned at the thought.

He moved the bacon slices with the spatula, saying in a sarcastic, sing-song voice, "This little piggie went to market, this little piggie stayed home, this little piggie is Joe's breakfast…"

A flaming-haired young woman who snapped, "Friends, not food," interrupted him from the breakfast bar."

Mari looked with gratitude at Heather Abbot, a nerdy young woman in their graduate student ranks. Heather was vegan, and having another plant-based eater nearby was a relief.

"No thanks," Mari answered him. She rested her hand lightly on her stomach. "I think I'll make some avocado toast. Join me?" she asked, turning to Heather with a smile.

"I would love some," Heather answered and gave Joe a searing look.

He shrugged and returned to his carnivore breakfast while the girls prepared their avocado toast. On the other hand, Nepeta sat at Joe's feet looking forlorn and gave an occasional, plaintive meow. Joe plated his food and glanced down at the cat. He tore off a small bite of bacon and blew on it before putting it on the floor for Nepeta, who gobbled it hungrily. Joe sat at the kitchen table, a bit away from the girls, who happily peeled and mashed the avocado and topped it with everything bagel seasoning. Nepeta followed him and sat beside him, looking up at Joe with big eyes, begging for another treat.

Others drifted down the stairs. Ren Lee, a flamboyant young man from Taiwan, yawned extravagantly. Nichelle White practically hopped down the stairs and bathed them in a smile. Franklin Dixon and Sunny Calista came down the stairs next. Sunny was bouncy, and Franklin looked determined. Lastly, Peter Hollister came down the stairs slowly, yawning and scratching at his belly.

Finally, Franklin cleared his throat, "What do you think we have in store for us today?"

"Probably orientation of some sort," Nichelle stated.

"I hope we can work in the gardens," Mari sighed. "Work in the garden, then classes. Isn't that the drill?"

Joe said cynically, "After all, we *are* the 21st-century version of indentured servants as well as being students."

"Yeah, garden work, class, and homework,"

Peter added.

"But, we're here," Mari sighed happily, "at Meadowood."

They all got quiet for a minute. Mari looked around the large table. Everyone was smiling and nodding. Nepeta meowed to break the silence, and they all laughed.

"Hey, I thought animals weren't allowed in the dorm?" Ren said.

"I won't tell if you won't," Heather said pointedly.

He shrugged in response.

"Hey, we have that reception tonight," Peter commented. "Some muckety-muck from across the pond is giving a lecture."

Joe groaned and asked, "formal?"

"Dunno," Peter answered.

"Look at the time," Nichelle told everyone. "We need to get to the potting shed. We'll surely get more details. Are we supposed to work in the gardens until 9:30, then off to class?"

"Yeah, and then a quick lunch, more work in class or lab, and homework," Peter complained.

They worked together and quickly rinsed and put their dishes and silverware in the dishwasher.

"C'mon, Nepeta, it's time to head outdoors," Mari told the huge cat. She picked up the big teddy bear of a cat, gave him a huge hug, and then put him on the ground after she stepped out of the dormitory into the morning sunshine. Nepeta sat at her feet, looked up at Marigold expectantly, and gave a plaintive meow, asking to be let inside again.

"It's time for your work too, Nepeta," Mari told the cat. "Go and keep nasty critters out of the garden. Let the garden visitors pet you. Shoo now."

She brushed her hands in the air as if to move the cat

along. He turned and stalked away from Mari, tail held high and switching at the top. If he could talk, Mari was certain he would say, "I'll be back."

She smiled as Nichelle, Heather, and Sunny caught up with her.

Sunny said, "I hope I can work in the Physick or Herb Gardens by the mansion today."

She had worked at her family's large-scale herb farm in California. She was head-over-heels, passionately in love with herbs.

Heather rolled her eyes before she looked at Nichelle.

"I don't care where I work," Nichelle said, "I'm just happy to be here." She glanced over at Mari, smiling in comradeship.

There was a loud whoop behind them. A large body rushed past them. Joe.

"Watch out! Incoming!" They heard Peter yell.

A small football whizzed past the girls so closely it riffled Mari's hair. Joe caught the football and ran with it, yelling, "Touchdown!" when he reached the border of the formal French gardens.

"Boys," Nichelle groaned, shaking her head.

The other girls agreed.

"Well…most of them," Sunny commented.

Mari glanced back. Franklin and Ren were in deep conversation and were coming along more slowly.

They walked around the Celtic Knot labyrinth rather than through it to reach the rear of the huge conservatory. It was an imposing Victorian structure. Mari had read somewhere that it was like a cross between the Crystal Palace at the 1851 World's Fair and the Palm House at the Natural History Museum in Copenhagen.

Beneath the Conservatory, through an entrance

marked "Employees Only" was the Potting Shed. A tall, imposing woman with long, brown hair tied back in a loose ponytail closed her eyes in near worship of the large coffee she sipped. Dr. Fuller.

Her eyes opened when the group of students broke her reverie of the brewed beans. She didn't look overly happy but took another sip before reverently setting the cup down.

"Good morning, saplings," she said with a slight edge to her voice. "Gather round."

Mari had learned Dr Fuller was an expert dendrologist and passionate about bonsai. Her expertise, reputation, and height, topping nearly six feet, made her imposing. Mari, a petite five-foot-one-inch, felt awed and cowed in her presence. Dr. Fuller called the graduate students saplings, sprouts, twigs, or scions, always with a sarcastic edge. Mari didn't think she meant to be mean, but rather funny. She wasn't sure. It didn't bother her. She took a deep breath, inhaling the rich scents of potting soil and green plants. Sunshine was slanting through the greenhouse windows, giving everything a golden glow. Mari sighed happily and turned her attention back to Dr. Fuller.

"You'll be spread through the gardens today, working on weeding and tending the beds."

"Be sure to pay attention to the required plant signs. Learn them, memorize them, and know their locations in the garden. Be sure to know the genus, scientific epithet, cultivar, common name, trademark name, native origin, and range of each plant.

Peter sighed audibly and whined, "Oh, man!" in a stage whisper.

"Is there a problem, Mr. Hollister?" Dr. Fuller asked, giving him a pointed stare.

Peter shifted his feet uncomfortably before answering, "No, ma'am."

"I'll assign you to various areas in the garden and drop by to see how you're doing. Everything should be cleaned up and shipshape by nine-forty-five. Ensure your tools are away and there's no trace of you. Guests should think the fairies were working all night to create garden magic. You," she pointed to each of them, "are part of the magic fairy tribe that works here."

She took a long sip of coffee and continued, "You'll have a class with Dr. Knight and then clean yourselves up for the reception and lecture for our esteemed guest, Dr. Alexander Wellington, Esquire."

There was a loud crash. Dr. Fuller stopped talking. Everyone turned. Franklin was beet red.

"Sorry, prof," he stammered. He bent down to pick up the shards from a terracotta pot.

"What happened?" Dr. Fuller asked, her eyes boring into Franklin's.

"I don't know. I must have been too close, and accidentally bumped it from the potting table."

"I'll help you," Ren said and went to get a trash can and a broom.

Dr. Fuller sighed, "As I was saying, we have a special guest this evening. I'm sure you'll all be fascinated with his research. He will also lecture for your class tomorrow. This is a good opportunity for you to get your feet wet in the professional world of botany. You are welcome to wear street clothes instead of your Meadowood uniform. Please be neat and clean."

Moments later, Mari breathed in the scents of the colorful rainbow of blossoms on the Flower Garden Walk. It was a river of color, scent, and blooms at their peak, bordered by boxwood defining the walk. The students' job was keeping everything in pristine shape at peak bloom. Mari had her snippers out and sheared off spent blossoms. Nichelle had a notepad and was making a list of plants that needed replacing. Sunny and Heather pulled out a long hose and began to water.

The day was warming up, and Mari, in her rush that morning, wished she had remembered sunscreen and her hat. Two hours of this and she would be as red as her hair. She sighed, pulling her collar up to protect her neck. She glanced over at the Clock Tower at the end of the walk. Surrounding the Clock Tower were small understory trees and large bushes. Mari stared at the shade longingly. That would be the place to be weeding today. There were beautiful seasonal flowers in front of the bushes. Tall blue salvia, bright orange marigolds, and brilliant garnet begonias were a bright splash of color against the mottled greens of a thick hedge of Aucuba under Dogwood and Crape Myrtle trees. She gave a last longing look at the shade and continued her task.

Mari focused on the plants, carefully pruning the flowers to look their best. She found herself getting lost in the color of the blossoms and stamens and noticing the variations in each. She was surprised when Nichelle called her name.

"Time to clean up, girlfriend. We have class soon."

Mari glanced up at the clock tower. The clock chimed the half hour. She had fifteen minutes to clean up and then go to the classrooms on the second floor of the Visitors Center.

"Let me help you," Nichelle told her. "Heather is helping Sunny with the behemoth of a hose."

"I lost track of time," Mari said faintly.

"Girl, you were in the zone," Nichelle laughed. "Sunny was the only one complaining because she wanted to be stationed in the gardens where the boys were assigned."

They hurriedly gathered everything, put tools away in the potting shed, and raced towards the Visitors Center.

"Did Dr. Fuller come by?" Mari panted as they hurried along.

"Nope," Nichelle said. "And I, for one, am glad. That woman is intimidating."

"You're not kidding."

They slowed down as they neared the Visitors' Center, an enormous crescent-shaped building. The downstairs held ticketing, a gift shop, a small theater, and a café. Upstairs held the administration offices and the educational classrooms. The inside of the crescent was tinted glass that featured the vista of the famous Blackthorn Cove and the Chesapeake Bay. It was a breathtaking sight, but they didn't have time to linger and admire the view.

"C'mon," Nichelle urged her. "I think we're the last to arrive."

The two women burst into the classroom. Mari could hear the clock tower chiming as she slid into her seat. She looked guiltily up at Dr. Knight sitting in a tall chair at the front of the classroom. Beside him was a cane. Rumor had it the cane was from a tree on the grounds of Buckingham Palace. It was carved with intricate symbols and leaves. He nodded at their entrance.

He sat patiently and listened for the clock to strike ten. He then turned a brilliant smile to his students.

"Welcome to week two of 'Plant Propagation.' I trust you had time to read the first three chapters in our riveting textbook, *Plant Propagation, and Practice*, over the weekend. I also trust you were able to email me your dialectical journals on said chapters. If not, please do so soon, as they will be marked as late after midnight tonight. I will review your journals and make comments within the week. Today, we will discuss plant propagation as a means of conservation. Why is this important? How do we do this?"

He looked at the students, raised an eyebrow, and waited. The students were quiet. Ren was scribbling in his notebook. Peter scratched his new sunburn. Franklin looked interested in contributing, but he also looked tongue-tied. Mari raised her hand tentatively.

"Yes, Mari?" Dr. Knight looked relieved and smiled at her.

She smiled back. She was hesitant to participate fully in his class. No one in the program knew that Dr. Knight was a personal acquaintance of her grandfather's. She didn't know him. She had stories from her grandfather but didn't want it to seem like she was brown-nosing the professor with her familiarity.

Her voice wavered at first, "Plant propagation as conservation is first and foremost a way to save plant species from extinction. Gardens like Meadowood have been integral in propagating rare and endangered plants so that we can ensure their survival despite climate change, habitat destruction, or invasive species."

"Correct," Dr. Knight answered enthusiastically, "and..."

Franklin found his voice, "Seed banks. The Svalbard Global Seed Vault was created to keep tens of thousands of varieties of seeds, especially vital food crops, safe."

"Very good," Dr. Knight praised Franklin. "We bank our seeds and propagate these plants to reintroduce them to the population. We depend on preserving genetic diversity in plants and monitoring and protecting these plants in botanical gardens like Meadowood. So... Meadowood is *not* just a pretty face. We, and other botanical gardens, do good, no great work, in conserving the planet's species. My next question is, how do we accomplish this?"

In a bored tone, Ren said, "We've talked about seed banks. We can also take cuttings, do tissue culture, divide plants, and join plants through grafting."

Mari glanced back at him. Ren's expression was somewhere between boredom and sullenness.

"Excellent, Ren," Dr. Knight stated.

Dr. Knight went on to discuss each point at great length. Mari found herself scribbling note after note. She would need to go back and organize them later. He talked very quickly. She had to listen carefully to catch every word.

After an hour of solid lecturing, there was a knock at their classroom door. Mari recognized the woman who entered as the department secretary. It was Janet Adams, with a short, gray bob and large purple glasses perched on her nose. She was quite thin and had a cardigan on despite the warm day. She went over to Dr. Knight, apologizing.

"May I speak with you privately, Dr. Knight?" she inquired.

"Of course," Dr. Knight said benevolently. "Let's step out in the hall, shall we?"

He followed her out the door.

"Nice to have a little break," Heather commented. "I think my hand was going to fall off from all the notes I was taking."

"Same," Mari agreed.

Sunny yawned, "I know I've been on the East Coast for a week, but my body is still on West Coast time. Getting up this morning was like getting up in the middle of the night. I could use a nap."

A few minutes passed. Dr. Knight returned and cleared his throat before stating, "I seem to be needed elsewhere and must cut this class a trifle short. You are released until one o'clock sharp for our lab time. I'll go over hands-on methods for each of the propagation methods."

He strode out the door, his cane clacking almost staccato.

"He seems annoyed," Nichelle commented. "I wonder what's happening?"

"I don't care," Peter said, "It's groovy to get an extra hour. I'm going to get some lunch back at the dorm and take a nap."

"That sounds like an excellent plan," Sunny agreed.

Mari went back to the dorm with the group. She wanted a shower more than lunch after perspiring in the sun. She turned the shower to lukewarm to keep her sunburn from stinging. Grateful that her mom gifted her a large aloe plant, she broke off a spiky leaf and squeezed the gel to rub on her sunburned skin. It was sticky but cooled the burn right away. She felt drowsy, too, and vowed not to lie on the bed.

Instead, she perched in the window seat in her room and looked out at the garden. Tourists were milling about. It was a beautiful day. She was lost in reverie until a loud knock pulled her from her pleasant morning memories.

"Come in," she called.

Heather opened the door, bearing two bowls. " Would you like to share my awesome chickpea salad with me?"

"Thanks. That sounds amazing."

Heather handed Mari a bowl of colorful salad topped

with a hunk of crusty French bread before sitting in the small upholstered armchair that faced the windows.

"You have a great view here," she commented before taking a bite of the salad.

Mari nodded, her mouth full of garbanzos and vegetables. "I know," she finally admitted, "I don't know how I got so lucky. Your salad is fantastic. Thank you."

Heather nodded. "I like my view too. I'm facing the woods, and it's almost like being in a treehouse."

"That's cool."

"So, propagation this afternoon."

It was Mari's turn to nod, "I'm glad it's something familiar."

"For you, maybe," Heather said, scoffing. "Can I be your lab partner? I worked with plants but never propagated them."

"Of course. It's pretty easy. This is where they're starting us off with the basics before we get into the nitty-gritty of garden administration."

"Yeah, and it's something we can also work at as the Meadowood free labor."

"True," Mari agreed. "And, we'll be able to work with some great plants. Some of them are probably endangered. It will be fun."

"If you say so. Let's get going. I don't want to be late."

They returned to the Visitors Center to another classroom area set up as a lab. This time, they were the first to arrive. The others trickled in. Sunny looked a little rumpled but more awake.

"You must have gotten your nap," Mari commented.

Sunny gave her a bright smile and nodded in return.

The clock tower struck one o'clock. There was no professor. That was odd. Mari knew he was a prompt man and expected his students to be on time as well.

A few more minutes passed. There was no Dr. Knight. They were chatting quietly, but everyone kept glancing at the door.

Peter had his eyes on the clock above the door. "What's that rule? Fifteen minutes, and then we can go? Wouldn't it be awesome to have the afternoon off to chill?"

The minutes ticked by, and everyone's eyes were on the clock. No Dr. Knight.

CHAPTER TWO

At one fourteen, the staccato clack of Dr. Knight's cane could be heard outside the lab. He entered, looking disheveled and a little distraught. Mari wondered what had happened. He didn't explain. Instead, he launched into the different ways to propagate plants. He seemed to be slightly anxious, and he was talking very fast. It wasn't easy to keep up.

Dr. Knight demonstrated the different ways to propagate and then told them to practice themselves. He expected them to write and send their notes to him, but he told the class he needed to leave. He apologized but distractedly and vaguely said, "I'll see you later this evening."

"What was that all about?" Ren asked. "Weird."

They all agreed. Most of the other students hurried through their practice and notes. Heather looked worried. Mari showed her each step slowly and carefully, giving Heather time to take notes and ask questions.

"Thanks," she told Mari, breathing a sigh of relief as they cleaned up.

Everyone else had gone.

"What are you wearing tonight?" Heather asked. "It's cool we can wear street clothes."

"Umm, I haven't decided yet. I think a sundress my grandmother sent me. It's pretty and will be comfortable to wear in the heat. I think summer is officially here."

"Yeah, I wonder what the air-conditioning is like in the old mansion? Most of those older places don't take well to modern conversions. I hope that they have some vegan options at the reception. If not, I'll head back to the dorm for more chickpea salad."

"That was delicious. Thanks again for bringing me lunch. I'll need to get your recipe for the dressing. It was creamy. What is your secret?"

Heather laughed, "Tahini in a basic lemon vinaigrette," she commented as they packed up to return to the dorm. "It's my trade secret, so 'shh.'"

"I won't tell, I promise."

They laughed and chatted back to the dorm. Nepeta was waiting outside. When they arrived at the door, he meowed plaintively. Both women laughed. Nepeta rubbed against Mari's legs.

"All right, all right, you can come in."

Once the door was open, Nepeta raced inside and up the stairs. He was waiting for Mari to open her door. Inside her room, he jumped up on the window seat and turned around and around until he was settled in a spot of the bright afternoon sun streaming in the window.

"You're going to turn into a baked cat lying there," Mari warned.

Nepeta opened one eye briefly, meowed softly, and closed his eyes again. Mari sat at her desk and opened her notebook and laptop. She wanted to write up her notes and send them off to Dr. Knight as soon as possible. That way, she could go to the reception and lecture with a clear conscience.

Tongue between her teeth, Mari read through her notes, editing them as she went along. She typed them for herself and then copied and sent them to Dr. Knight. She remembered his passion in voicing to the students that Meadowood prided itself on conservation horticulture, greenhouse and crop production, land stewardship, and ecology. He mentioned the Meadowood publications and urged them, during their tenure, to think about researching to advance horticultural science. She liked his enthusiasm for Meadowood and plants.

Looking at the clock, she was surprised that the afternoon had passed quickly and that it was time to get ready for the reception at the Blackthorn mansion.

She hoped her sundress was appropriate for the evening. She pulled it from the closet. Her grandparents lived in Britain, and her grandmother frequently sent Mari, her sister, and her mom lovely clothes with Liberty prints and more. This dress's fabric was based on the "Trailing Marigold" print. It was a sheath dress of bright Robin's egg blue patterned with subtle leafy vines with bright yellow flowers. She pulled a pair of heeled sandals from under her bed, brushed her hair until it shone, and added dangling silver marigold blossom earrings. Fortunately, the dress had pockets, and Mari could carry the key to her room. She left her phone charging on her desk and went to the common area to wait for the others. One by one, the students came and duly admired one another in fancier duds. They walked, as a group, toward the Blackthorn Mansion.

The Blackthorn Mansion looked magnificent in the late afternoon sunshine. Made of local granite embedded with a multitude of mica, it almost sparkled in the sun. Inside, Mari admired the sweeping, curving staircase carved with the blossoms of Prunus Spinosa, Blackthorn, carved into the Newell post. The Newell post and balustrades were carved from dark Blackthorn wood, and the remainder of the staircase was walnut. The darker woods used in the staircase were stunning against the creamy, light backdrop of the walls. They walked past the staircase to the formal dining room. It was a large expanse of a room restored to the fashion of 1860. It had been electrified, but several candelabras graced the table and gave off a warm glow with the candlelight. The table was heavily laden with food.

A long sideboard held steaming trays of hot appetizers, and a bar was set up at the end that led to a covered porch area. It was cleverly designed, as the tall windows were lowered to the basement to leave open doorways to lead outside. Once guests had food and drink, they meandered to a verandah and down the steps, where small chairs and tables were strewn over the lawn near the formal French gardens.

Mari's stomach growled at the sight of the food. She picked up a plate and loaded it with delicacies. She was happy to see some seafood and many vegetable options. Plate loaded, she stopped by the bar. She asked about cider and was given a blank look. She sighed. Her grandparents had a small cidery in the county of Sussex in the United Kingdom called "The Monk's Last Drop." Their ciders were award-winning. Their good stuff was only available locally. She wasn't expecting it here but knew cideries were growing in popularity and knew of a local one. She was disappointed and settled for a glass of Pinot Noir.

She walked outside, smiling shyly at the guests she didn't know. They were likely Meadowood Board members or Garden Pass holders of the highest level. The Garden Pass holders were prestigious members of the garden community who donated large amounts of money to the botanic garden. It was a lovely evening. The day's heat had dissipated, and the breeze perfumed the air with a medley of scents from the Flower Garden Walk. Gratefully, she joined the other students hovering around two adjoining tables. They were a quiet crowd as they sipped their drinks and nibbled on their food.

"Uh, oh," Franklin commented as Dr. Fuller strode towards them.

Dr. Fuller, lovely in deep blue palazzo pants and a floaty chiffon tunic, looked determined. She wore a large silver leaf on a long chain. Something sparkled in her ears. She snapped her fingers at them, stating, "Scions, it's time to mingle. I don't want to see you clumped together like a bunch of berries. Go forth! Introduce yourselves! Be proud you are on the Meadowood team."

Mari gulped some of her wine. She looked at her fellow students, who mostly looked like deer in headlights.

"Go!" Dr. Fuller ordered again.

They scattered, and Mari wasn't sure where to go. She tried to balance her wine and her plate and wanted to eat a little food. Ren breezed past, looking dapper in a crisp white shirt and creamy linen pants slung a little low on his hips. He almost looked like a dandy from the Roaring 20s with his dark hair slicked back.

"Nice Liberty print you're wearing," he commented in passing. "The colors look good on you."

She was taking a sip of her wine when the unexpected compliments came from Ren. She swallowed and almost sputtered a thank you, but he was already gone. You couldn't really tell much about Ren. He was sarcastic most of the time, but his comments to Mari seemed genuine.

She inadvertently shrugged her shoulders while taking another sip of wine and backed up into a very tall man. His hair was salt and pepper, and Mari guessed he was in his forties. Mari recognized him; he was Jonathan Howard, the bookstore owner of The Last Page in the nearby town of Oak Harbor. She and her family had spent many a happy hour there. He caught her by the elbow and kept her from spilling her wine and food.

"Whoa, easy there," he said.

"I am so sorry," Mari apologized, "I'm sorry, Mr. Howard."

"Do I know you?"

Mari flushed, "Probably not. My family and I frequent your wonderful bookstore when we come to Meadowood. I'm Marigold Saille. I'm a graduate student here at Meadowood."

"Oh!" Mr. Howard answered, and he studied her. "I *do* remember you. You have a brother and sister, correct? He likes sci-fi, and she likes mysteries, right?"

"Right!"

"And you," he paused, "plants and folklore."

"Yes," Mari admitted, "My whole family loves books. My parents never wanted us to pick up tchotchkes from the Meadowood gift shop, so they promised us a book instead. Thus, we frequented your store quite often."

"Well, tell your parents 'thank you'. What a grand idea."

"How is McTavish?" Mari asked.

McTavish was the Scottish Deerhound that lived at the bookstore. It wasn't unusual for a kid to be snuggled up with McTavish or for McTavish to sit at your feet while you read. It also wasn't unusual to see McTavish carrying a basket of books to the counter for patrons.

"He's just fine. I will give him your regards later this evening."

"He's a wonderful dog."

"That he is. So, you're a graduate student, eh? What's that like?"

"Wonderful," she breathed. "I've just finished my first week. We're all working on our Master's program in Public Garden Administration."

"That sounds impressive, but only one week?"

"Yes, sir."

"Well, very good luck to you. I look forward to seeing you in the store when you get a chance to come into town."

"Thank you, Mr. Howard."

Mr. Howard went back inside.

Mari looked around. People were milling about, but she couldn't see Heather or Nichelle in the crowd. She did see Sunny. She was striking with her long, blond hair streaming down her back. In a turquoise halter maxi dress, she was deeply conversing with a man in a suit. Sunny reminded her of a flower child. A waiter walked by with a tray, and Mari put her empty glass and plate on it, thanking the man.

Ren looked upset and different from the stoic mask he usually wore. He was talking to a gentleman in a tailored suit on the other side of the room. She wondered what he was upset about. Who would he know here in the States at this little gathering? It was odd.

Then she spied Dr. Knight—finally, a familiar face. Mari started to walk towards him when she saw Joe stop Dr. Knight. He looked upset, too. What was with everyone tonight? Dr. Knight kept shaking his head. Joe was getting visibly distressed and trying to keep his voice down. Dr. Knight held up a hand to stop the conversation, used his cane, and raised it in the air, pointing towards the mansion.

Mari looked up at the clock tower. It was time for the lecture. Everyone had disappeared into the mansion. She hurried and slid into a seat at the back of the crowded parlor.

Dr. Knight approached the podium and introduced Dr. Alexander Wellington, Esquire, as a colleague and challenging rival in the world of botany. He said it with a smile that didn't reach his eyes. Dr. Wellington gave him a sharp glance but recovered quickly. Dr. Wellington wasn't an overly tall man, He was slightly portly and rested one hand on his small paunch. He had dark, wavy hair and an air of self-importance. He seemed to smirk at Dr. Knight, and that put Mari off.

He began in a clipped voice, one her grandmother would have said came from the upper crust of British society, "Dr. Seuss stated in the book *The Lorax,* *"I speak for the trees."* I can tell you that I speak for the bees. What does that mean? Some of you may be familiar with my work with heaths and heathers. I have recently been researching how the nectar from Calluna Vulgaris kills the common parasite, Crithidia bombi. As you know, bees and other pollinators are critical for our planet's survival. In recent years, bees have been battling habitat loss and destruction by pollutants and serious parasites that kill entire colonies. A compound from Calluna Vulgaris – Callunene, will inhibit this parasite in bumblebees."

Dr. Wellington described in detail the research undertaken at London's Kew Gardens and his own University. Mari was interested, but he seemed to drone on, talking about his accomplishments at length. She looked around. She wasn't the only one bored. One man was clearly asleep. Others were checking their phones. She saw a few trying to hide yawns. Her fellow students were also looking bored, except Heather, who was passionate about insects and integrated pest management.

Mari stifled her own yawn. She could see out the window that overlooked the cove and bay. The sun was setting, sending golden and apricot light through the sky and over the water. Mari was enchanted by the sight and was lost in the vista until polite applause pulled her away from the colors.

When the applause ended, Mari stood, refraining from the wish to yawn and stretch. She waited at the rear of the parlor for Heather, Nichelle, and Sunny. Peter and Franklin joined them. Mari didn't see Ren or Joe.

The sunset had turned to twilight, and darkness quickly followed. The six of them walked through the formal French gardens where long shadows created puddles of darkness. Mari had always dreamed of being alone in the gardens, but this was a little creepy. She glanced around nervously, happy to be with her companions.

Mari went up to her room, where Nepeta was waiting for her. She got comfortable in her pajamas, turned out the lights, and sat in the window seat with her laptop and a purring cat. A soft breeze blew through her open windows. It held the scent of water mixed with green and floral notes. Mari closed her eyes briefly, thinking it would make a lovely perfume.

She accessed the list of required plants and worked to memorize each one. Then, with her tongue between her teeth, she wondered if she could make flashcards. She searched for a program to help her with this. When she found one, she started plugging in photographs of each plant and the information she needed.

Outside, she heard a Screech Owl hooting from the

forest. It was a haunting sound. Then, she thought she heard a fox scream. But was it a fox? It sounded odd and different from any fox sound she was familiar with, but she couldn't be sure. She listened again, instinctively closing her laptop, letting the darkness settle around her.

Mari looked out over the dark gardens. She thought she saw movement. Was someone out there? If so, who? She squinted, trying to see better. It was of no use. The gardens were dark. She stilled when she heard someone rummaging around in the common area. Maybe someone was getting a snack. In the distance, Mari heard a car door slam and the engine start. Was it in the Meadowood parking lot? How odd at this time of night, but then sounds carried differently near the water. She couldn't be sure where the sound came from. She froze when the owl hooted again with a loud, whinnying sound.

Nepeta's soft paw on her leg made her jump. He wanted her to go to bed.

"Okay, okay," she whispered to the insistent cat.

Mari didn't know why she was whispering but climbed into bed, grateful for Nepeta's company.

CHAPTER THREE

Nepeta was better than any alarm. His rough, scratchy tongue on her nose woke her up immediately. She gently pushed the cat aside to glance at her phone. It was fifteen minutes before her alarm would ring, so she turned it off. The early sunshine lit up the room, chasing away any shadows.

Brilliant sunshine foretold another hot day. Mari slathered herself with sunscreen and put on her gardening sleeves and Boonie hat to combat sunburn. Down in the common area, she rummaged through her assigned cupboard to locate a small can of baked beans. Beans on toast was a childhood favorite. She was feeling comfort food.

"Beans on toast. Good choice!" Ren commented, "Have you been to England?"

"Every year," Mari said after she finished a bite. "My grandparents live in the UK. I go as often as I can."

"Cool."

Mari was surprised Ren knew about beans on toast. She was about to ask him if he had been to England and how he knew of the breakfast dish, but Joe looked at her plate and made gagging sounds. Mari rolled her eyes instead, and Ren stalked away, equally disgusted with Joe's reaction.   When they arrived at the potting shed, Dr. Fuller was in rare form. She barked orders at them and assigned Mari, Joe, Peter, and Heather to weed and trim the formal French gardens, while Nichelle, Sunny, Ren, and Franklin were assigned to work on the Sensory Garden.

The parterres were surrounded by clipped boxwood and had colorful and sweet-smelling heliotropes, sharp-smelling pelargoniums, spicy petunias, and brilliant salvias. The gravel walks were close to immaculate and Joe began raking to keep them that way. Mari took a deep breath, enjoying the scents, even the smell of the boxwood. She looked up and around. Parterres were to be seen and enjoyed from above and strolling on the walkways. She looked up at the mansion and wondered how the view was from the second floor. Visitors and tourists never had access to the second floor of the mansion. She always wondered what was there. Now, at Meadowood full-time, she understood it housed the private library and offices of Lord and Lady Blackthorn. She had previously climbed the clock tower and admired the gardens from the balcony.

"Hey, girlfriend, are you going to work?" Heather asked gently. "Dr. Fuller threatened to come and watch over us today."

"Sorry," Mari replied. I became lost in thought. I was wondering how these gardens looked from the mansion's second floor. I wonder if we can check that out someday."

"Yeah, I think the turret was Lady Blackthorn's sitting room back in the day. What a pretty sight it must be from up there."

"That's what I was thinking. I've seen it from the clock tower, and it's amazing. It reminds me of the pictures I've seen of the gardens of Versailles and Drummond Castle. My grandparents took my family to Drummond Castle and Gardens in Scotland on one of our visits. You'll have to Google it. The gardens were built in the 17th century."

They continued to chat as they weeded and clipped. Just as the clock struck eight, Nepeta came into the garden and meowed at Mari.

"Hello, sweetie," she crooned and bent down to pet and hug the large cat.

Nepeta didn't want to be petted. He meowed, turned, and walked away, but circled back, repeating the behavior over and over.

"I wonder what's wrong with him?" Mari asked.

"He wants you to follow him," suggested Heather.

The next time he circled back and meowed at Mari, he turned and ran a few steps forward. He repeated the behavior and led Mari out of the garden.

"Are you sure you want to follow the cat? Dr. Fuller will be here any second. What will she say when you're not here? She was pretty grumpy this morning. I think she forgot her coffee," Heather said worriedly.

"I'll just be a minute. Maybe there's a dead bird or something."

Mari turned back to the cat. "I'm coming, Nepeta."

He gave a satisfied meow in response and trotted away. Mari followed. She heard a shout behind her. It was Dr. Fuller.

"Ms. Saille, where are you going? You can't shirk!" came Dr. Fuller's voice in a shrill tone.

"I'll be back in a minute!' Mari called back.

She couldn't hear Dr. Fuller's words but knew they weren't happy.

Nepeta led her out of the French Gardens. Occasionally, Nepeta would look over his shoulder and meow at Mari as if to say, "Hurry up!" He led her to the path around the clock tower. The creamy blossoms of the Kousa dogwoods were in full bloom, stark against the tower's granite.

Nepeta became more insistent. He meowed loudly, stopping and waiting for Mari to catch up before moving forward.

"What is it, boy?"

Nepeta meowed and then gave a loud yowl, which made Mari shiver. He led her past the annuals on the outer edge of the clock tower gardens. Mari stepped carefully so as not to crush any plants. The Japanese Aucuba grew thickly. Nepeta scooted under one of the bushes, stopped, and yowled again.

"I'm coming, Nepeta. I need to be careful of the plantings." She carefully parted the leaves between two bushes, and her foot bumped into something firm and soft. *Odd*, she thought, and then she looked.

Lying on the ground was Dr. Wellington. His body was askew at an odd angle, wedged between the Aucuba and the trunk of a dogwood tree. Some blossoms had drifted on top of him, and there was a pool of something dark on the soil. It looked like blood. Mari froze. And then, she screamed.

Disregarding the plantings, she burst from the Clock Tower Garden and screamed for help over and over. Sunny, Nichelle, and Franklin came running. Ren followed.

"What's wrong, Mari?" Nichelle approached Mari and touched her arm to steady her. Mari's eyes were wide with fright. Mari couldn't stop screaming. Nichelle took her other arm and squeezed hard. Sunny and Franklin hovered.

"Mari. Stop. Look at me. Tell me what's wrong," Nichelle said calmly. She gave Mari a small shake.

Her screams stopped, and babbling sounds emerged from her.

"Mari, what's wrong?" Sunny asked her, a little impatient.

"Dr. Wellington," Mari gulped. "Dr. Wellington is lying over there. I think I think he's dead."

Franklin's head jerked in the direction of the tower. "Where?"

Mari pointed a shaking finger, "Over there."

"Someone needs to get help. Ren, find Dr. Fuller. I think she's in the French Gardens. Sunny, call 911," Nichelle gave snapping orders.

Franklin started to approach the tower.

"Franklin, we can't go in there. It's probably a crime scene, even if it's suicide. We need to wait for the police," Nichelle warned.

"I need to see if he's okay. Maybe he needs CPR." Franklin carefully stepped over the annual plantings and pushed through the Aucuba. He, too, froze in his tracks. He bent down and disappeared for a moment with his arm outstretched. He stood up, gray-faced.

Mari saw Franklin's face and scrunched her eyes closed. She swayed. Nichelle grabbed her.

"Mari, come sit on this bench. Franklin, help me."

Franklin returned to the girls. Nichelle and Franklin each took one of Mari's arms and led her to a semi-circular bench that faced the Flower Garden Walk. It was called the Whispering Bench and was similar to the ones at Longwood Gardens, Central Park, and Philadelphia. One person could sit at one end of the bench and whisper into it, and the person at the other end could hear them. They didn't play that game now but rather sat in the center of the bench. Mari pulled her knees up to her chest. Nepeta came out of the Clock Tower Garden and strode to her, tail held high. He jumped up between Nichelle and Mari and rubbed his head on Mari's leg, purring.

Mari leaned over and kissed the top of the big cat's head. "Oh, Nepeta," she whispered.

Tears started to well up, but Dr. Fuller's approach quelled them.

"What's up, saplings? Why all the sitting around? Ren said there was an emergency. Is someone hurt? You look fine. What's that cat doing here?" she queried in her usual sharp-tongued manner. Her hands were on her hips.

Mari looked up at her and cleared her throat. "Dr. Wellington. He's back there. By the tower. I think he's dead."

"What?" Dr. Fuller scoffed. "Where?"

Mari pointed.

"I checked, Dr. Fuller. He's dead," Franklin corroborated.

"Sunny called 911," Nichelle said helpfully.

"Franklin, show me," Dr. Fuller commanded.

Franklin took Dr. Fuller to the site where Dr. Wellington lay. She put her hand to her mouth.

"Oh, my God!" She breathed loudly in a stage whisper.

The entire group of students was present now, along with Dr. Fuller. Dr. Fuller was on the phone with Meadowood's administration, informing them what had happened and that the police and EMTs were on their way. Everyone was quiet. Heads raised when they heard sirens. It took a few minutes for the EMTs and police to reach the clock tower. Franklin showed the EMTs where the body lay. They tested for a pulse, shook their heads, and backed off.

The police came and approached the group.

"Who's in charge here?" one of the cops asked the group.

Dr. Fuller stepped forward and said coolly, "I am. One of my students found Dr. Wellington's body by the Clock Tower."

"Which student?"

Dr. Fuller pointed at Mari. Mari stood shakily, gently putting Nepeta on the ground. The second cop noticed.

"Miss, just stay there." He turned and faced the group. "Can you move just a little way away? I need to speak with this young lady privately."

"We'll gather over there," Dr. Fuller pointed North. "In the Meditation Garden, there are several benches."

Dr. Fuller herded the group of students away. Nepeta followed. They were talking in whispers. Mari sat down on the bench again. She felt like a hollow stone. The cops approached Mari.

The taller one with dark brown hair and hazel eyes looked at her kindly, "I'm Detective John Booker. You found the deceased?"

Mari nodded.

The other cop was more brusque. He introduced himself as Detective Parker. He was older, maybe in his late forties. He had a bald spot and a shorter, more compact body. "Can you state your name, Ma'am, and tell us how you came to find the body?"

"Y-yes," Mari stammered. "I'm Marigold Saille. I'm a student here. Nepeta, one of the cats at Meadowood, led me to Dr. Wellington."

"A cat? Dr. Wellington? Do you know him?"

"No, not really. He's, or he was, a visiting lecturer here at Meadowood. He spoke last evening at an event and was going to be a guest at our class this afternoon."

"Do you know how he ended up by the tower?" Detective Parker interrupted.

Mari's eyes grew wide and round, "No! Nepeta was upset and kept meowing at me. I followed him here and found Dr. Wellington." She looked up into the faces of the cops, "How did he die?"

"We'll be investigating that."

"What Detective Parker is saying is that this is an ongoing investigation. You need to give us a few more details. What time did you find the professor?"

Mari answered, adding, "We start our day at 7:30 at the potting shed. I was in the French Gardens by 7:45. Nepeta came for me around eight. I remember hearing the clock chiming."

"What were you doing before you came to the potting shed and gardens?"

"Umm, I was back at the dorm with the other students. We were having breakfast."

"And what time did you last see Dr. Wellington?"

"About eight last night. He finished his lecture, and we went back to the dorm."

"I think that's all the questions we have for now. We'll walk you to the other students."

A voice from the Clock Tower area called, "Detectives, please come over here."

"Stay right there," Detective Parker ordered.

The detectives walked over to the forensics team that had arrived.

Mari couldn't help it; she looked toward the Clock Tower. One of the forensics team held something up that gleamed in the sunlight. It looked like a small sword. It looked familiar. Where had she seen it before? Her brain wasn't working the way it should. She couldn't remember.

"Bag it," she heard Detective Booker say. "Check it

for prints and test the blood."

Detectives Booker and Parker returned to Mari. They didn't frog march her to the other students, but they flanked her on either side. It made her nervous. When she reached everyone, Nichelle stood and hugged Mari. She pulled Mari down beside her on the bench. Heather sat on her other side. They heard Detective Parker tell Dr. Fuller that Mari would need to go to the station to give a formal statement. Detective Booker pulled each student aside and asked a few questions. They finished, thanked everyone, and returned to the Clock Tower, now marked off with Crime Scene tape.

"It's not much," she heard Detective Booker remark.

"But a cat showing the way?" she heard Detective Parker say disgustedly, "That's a new one."

And with that, Mari knew he didn't believe her by the tone of his voice. And she wondered what that meant.

CHAPTER FOUR

Dr. Fuller led the group to the classroom area in the Visitors Center. She asked them to stay put in the classroom. She left and, a few minutes later, turned up with Dr. Knight. He looked shaken.

"We'll have to play the next few days out as we can," Dr. Fuller told the group. "Mari, you'll need to get to the police station in Oak Harbor to give a formal statement. Can you do that this afternoon?"

Mari nodded.

"Obviously, Dr. Wellington will not be lecturing today. If Dr. Knight agrees, we can give you the remainder of the day off to process Dr. Wellington's death, or if you prefer to keep busy, work on learning the required plants. This is a project for you to identify groupings of plants in various plant collections. You will learn more about the Meadowood collection and a good base collection for other botanical gardens. Sometime in the future, you will be tested on the knowledge. Be sure to focus on each plant's common name, the scientific name, including the generic and specific epithet. Also, you will need to memorize the cultivar name, the nativity of the species, as well as the common family name. Mari, you'll need to spend extra time outside of today to do this."

Dr. Knight nodded. He was rubbing his chin and tugging at his beard.

Heather raised her hand, "Would it be all right for me to accompany Mari to the police station?"

Mari sent Heather a grateful look.

"I think that would be all right. Progress on the required plants should be emailed to me by the end of the week. You are dismissed."

The group exited more quietly than usual. Franklin, Sunny, and Ren headed to the gardens with notebooks while Peter, Nichelle, Joe, Heather, and Mari walked toward the dorm.

Heather noticed Mari was still shaky and said, "I'll drive."

Joe looked at her quizzically, "what kinds of questions do you think they'll ask you?"

Mari shrugged. "I have no idea. I think the one cop thinks I'm lying when I said Nepeta led me to the body. But he did!" She turned to Heather. "Give me fifteen minutes to freshen up, okay? I think I want to get out of Meadowood clothes."

"Me too," Heather agreed. "What are you guys up to?" she asked Nichelle and Joe.

"Lunch," Joe responded as if it was obvious.

"And, then, out to identify plants. I want to keep busy," Nichelle said. She grimaced. "Good   luck," Heather laughed.

Fifteen minutes later, Mari had taken the quickest shower in her life and changed into lightweight chinos and a cotton peasant blouse. She met Heather in the common area, who was tossing her keys up in the air and catching them.

"Ready?" she asked Mari. "Let's go and get this done."

Mari nodded.

They walked to the employee parking lot, where Heather had a small car. She called it "Bugsy" because she called the color bug-gut green. It was an older model car, but Heather was fond of it.

The roads to Oak Harbor were small, two-lane roads that meandered through the countryside of soybean fields, carpenter Victorian farmhouses, and glimpses of plantations and estates along the bay. Oak Harbor was a charming Eastern Shore town. Many houses were white clapboard. There were several Victorian homes with an excess of gingerbread gracing the architecture. The town held a bookstore, a library, a bakery, a chocolate shop, a fifties-style diner, gift shops, and antique shops. There was a park in town that bordered the waterfront. A small museum that featured seasonal displays was off to the side. The police station was near the public library at the northern end of the town. The structure was mid-century modern, of brick and long, horizontal windows. Heather parked in a Visitor's spot, and they went inside.

Like most institutional buildings, the prevailing odor of disinfectant met them. A woman at the front desk asked how she could help them. Mari introduced herself and mentioned Detectives Booker and Parker. The woman asked them to sit. They did, in uncomfortable plastic chairs. Mari was still nervous.

"Chill, Mari," Heather whispered to her. "You've done nothing wrong. You found the body. You did them a favor. You didn't kill Dr. Wellington or force him into suicide. We don't know what happened."

"I forgot to tell you," Mari whispered back, "I saw

the Forensics team find a small sword thing near his body." She shivered at the memory. "It was covered in blood."

"Yikes!" Heather whispered.

She was about to say something more when Detective Booker came through a locked door.

"Thanks for coming so promptly, Ms. Saille. You can follow me."

He used his badge to open the door and waved her through. "Second door on the right," he told her.

Mari almost giggled in a bit of hysteria, thinking of the "second star to the right in *Peter Pan.*"

The second doorway led into a room with a table and a couple of chairs. There was a two-way mirror on one wall. Mari noticed cameras and microphones as well.

"Have a seat." Detective Booker told her and held the chair for her.

Mari sat. She was nervous, and her palms began to sweat. Trying to be unobtrusive, she wiped them carefully on her pants, brushed some hair out of her eyes, and then folded her hands on the table.

Detective Booker told Mari that she wasn't being charged but that they had a few questions that would be recorded. She would also be asked to write a formal statement.

"Please state your full name," Detective Booker asked Mari.

Clenching and unclenching her hands, she did so and answered the questions as best she could. Detective Booker asked her what she witnessed, requesting as many details as possible. He also asked about her relationship with Dr. Wellington. Mari felt like she was repeating herself from earlier that day.

Detective Booker continued with probing questions.

Mari was exhausted from the stress of the day and the situation.

Gritting her teeth to gain control of her emotions, she stated emphatically, "Detective Booker, I did not know Professor Wellington. I only saw him last night at the lecture. Nepeta was clearly agitated and led me to the body. I don't know what happened!"

"Do you have anything to add about last night?" Detective Booker continued to probe with questions.

Mari sat quietly, thinking. She added, "I was in my room, studying. I had the windows open. My lights were off, and Nepeta and I were sitting in the window seat. I heard an owl. I thought I heard a fox, but it sounded different. I thought I saw someone in the garden, but it was dark, and I couldn't see anything."

"What do you mean the fox sounded different?"

"Fox screams sound like people screaming, sometimes. It's such a weird sound. This one sounded different and a little far away. I questioned myself if I had really heard something."I think that's all for now," Detective Booker informed her. "I'll have you write up the incident. Also, here's my card if you think of anything else. We may need to ask you additional questions after we read your statement. We'll be in touch."

For the third time that day, Mari felt she was repeating herself as she wrote the report. When she was finished, she handed the signed report to Detective Booker. He thanked her and showed her to the lobby, where Heather was anxiously waiting.

Outside the police station Heather told her, "I didn't think you were ever getting out of there. Do you know you were there for over an hour and a half?"

"I am so tired," Mari complained. "I just want to crawl into bed and wake up pretending today never happened."

"But, you need some food. And you need to relax. Where can we eat in town?"

"There's a fifties-style diner, a high-end restaurant on the water, a bakery with good sandwiches, and an Irish-style pub."

"I don't know about you, but I vote for pub."

"I could use food and a drink," Mari said wearily.

The Lucky Penny was nearly bereft of patrons when they arrived. A guy at the bar was nursing a beer, and a couple was sitting in the back holding hands. The bartender told them to sit wherever they wanted, and Mari led Heather to a booth near a soot-stained river rock fireplace. It wasn't lit on this warm day, but she told Heather how lovely it was in the colder weather. The pub had hunter-green walls and dark wood furniture. It was almost cave-like but cozy.

When the bartender brought menus, they studied the offerings when the waitress came to take their orders. Heather ordered a Harp, and Mari ordered a Magners. They perused the menu. Mari suggested the Fish n' Chips but praised the Shepherd's Pie and Colcannon. Heather ordered Colcannon and Mari, a mushroom pie topped with mashed potatoes. When the waitress brought their drinks, they toasted to better days.

"So…" Heather began, "who offed Dr. Wellington? That's the elephant in the room. Unless it was suicide, eh? But why?"

Mari grimaced, "Not suicide from the small sword they found near his body James the blood on the ground. Who? I don't know. Who knows him other than Dr. Knight? And it couldn't have been him. He wouldn't hurt a fly."

"You never know about the quiet ones," Heather intoned. "But really, who would know him?"

"Maybe one of the Fellows? They're an international bunch. Maybe one of them worked with him. Do you think he wants to pin it on me since I found the body?" Mari questioned.

"That's ridiculous," Heather assured her.

"Maybe, but not so nearly far-fetched. That is if I knew Dr. Wellington. I told them I thought I heard someone in the gardens last night."

"Really?"

"Yeah. I sat in the window seat with Nepeta, looking at the required plants. My lights were out, but my windows were open. It sounded like someone was moving around, but maybe it was an animal."

"I heard an owl," Heather said. "At least, I think it was an owl."

"Did you hear a fox scream?"

"I'm not sure I would have recognized that. Anyway, I ended up taking a shower and heading to bed. I was wearing my earbuds and listening to a book."

"Hmmm...we're no closer than when we started."

Their food came. As hungry as Mari thought she was, she couldn't plow through the huge serving. She ended up asking for a box.

Heather scarfed her Colcannon, expressing how good it was to Mari between bites.

"Sorry, Heather, I am really tired," Mari apologized.

"It's okay, Mari. You've had a heck of a day. Look, I'll research who these Fellows are. Don't we have something else coming up socially where we can meet them?"

"Not sure. I think so. I want to go to bed and wake up tomorrow to start over. We need to figure out how to get around the garden to all those plants, too. Maybe tomorrow night? I started working on flashcards for each one. I'll share the file with you when I'm done. But first,

I want to show you one of my favorite places in Oak Harbor. You'll love it. It's a really great bookstore, and I know how you love books," she added slyly. "And this place will help me feel better. You'll see."

"Lead on," Heather told her.

They walked to the bookstore which was in an old church. The cavernous space was filled with oak bookshelves and squashy chairs. There was a coffee bar in the choir loft. Mari smiled as she watched Heather take it all in and laughed when Heather jumped when a cold nose touched her hand.

"Let me introduce you to McTavish, the co-owner of *The Last Page*. You can read with him, and he'll carry your books to the counter, too."

Mari knelt to hug the giant Scottish Deerhound while Heather patted his head.

"Oh, I needed you today, McTavish, more than you know," Mari whispered.

The dog followed them through the bookstore containing new and used titles. Behind the altar was a cozy children's book section with brightly colored rugs, bean bags, and a train table. Heather was impressed that the altar was still a thing in the bookstore."

"That's where he showcases great books. It's a unique marketing tool and a tongue-in-cheek thing," she explained to Heather.

Heather gave her a baleful look. "C'mon, let's get back to Meadowood. You look a little happier but still worn out."

Mari didn't disagree. She almost fell asleep in Bugsy on the return to Meadowood. Even though it was warm, Mari hoped Nepeta would snuggle with her that night. But Mari didn't sleep well. Images of Dr. Wellington's twisted body and the pool of dark blood that soaked into the soil gave her sleeping and waking nightmares. Mari's mind ran wild, wondering if he had been stabbed at the base of the Clock Tower or if someone had pushed him from the balcony of the Clock Tower or committed suicide.

Then, realization struck her. She remembered. The small sword she saw the cop hold up for the Detectives to see wasn't a sword at all. It was a letter opener belonging to Dr. Knight. At first, she couldn't remember where she had seen it, but now she did. She sat straight up in bed, thinking, 'No, no!' It wasn't possible. A shiver went down her spine, and she clutched at Nepeta, who protested with a sleepy meow. Should she tell the cops the letter opener belonged to Dr. Knight? She now remembered seeing it on his desk. If she didn't tell the police, wasn't that withholding information? She lay back, not knowing what to do.

CHAPTER FIVE

Mari tossed and turned the remainder of the night. Her alarm rang, and she hit the snooze three times. Finally, she turned off the alarm and lay in bed, fatigued by the dreams and insomnia of the night and by the realization of who owned the potential murder weapon. She lay back in bed, squeezing her eyes shut, willing the image of the letter opener to disappear.

There was a knock at her door.

"Just a minute," she called before swinging her legs out of bed. Nepeta protested.

When she opened the door, Heather had a cup of steaming coffee. She looked worried.

"How are you?"

"Come in," Mari invited and moved to the window seat, not answering Heather's question.

Heather followed her in and handed her the coffee.

"Thank you."

"How are you?" Heather asked again.

Mari shrugged, not trusting her voice or what to say.

She gratefully sipped the hot coffee instead.

"Do you want me to tell Dr. Fuller you're ill?"

"No!" Mari almost shouted. "I need to keep busy. I couldn't sleep. I just kept seeing Dr. Wellington's body over and over in my dreams. I'll go crazy if I'm here alone."

Nepeta came over and meowed.

Mari laughed ruefully, "Even if I was alone with you, Nepeta. I need to find something to keep me busy."

"Well then, I'll leave you to get dressed. See you downstairs," she said.

Mari dressed slowly, and as she did, she picked up and put down Detective Booker's card multiple times. Finally, she put it in her pocket. She called to Nepeta to follow her. He trailed behind her, tail held high. Everyone became quiet when she entered the common area.

"Good morning," she greeted everyone.

They responded with nods and quiet hellos.

Mari made herself a second cup of coffee and stared into her cupboard. She wasn't hungry but knew she should eat something.

"I'm having yogurt, berries, and granola if you're interested," Heather said helpfully.

"Sure," replied Mari. "Thanks."

She ate woodenly, not tasting the food. On the way to the Potting Shed, out of the corner of her eye, she saw the bright yellow of the crime scene tape still around the Clock Tower area. The yogurt and granola suddenly felt like rolling stones in her belly. She hesitated and began to trail behind, but Heather, Nichelle, and Sunny flanked her, supporting her as they continued to their meeting spot. Dr. Fuller was waiting inside.

Dr. Fuller stood for a minute, drinking her coffee. Looking at each student, her eyes softened with pity for

Mari. Mari looked back at her, feeling like her eyes were black holes in her face. She was sure she looked fatigued.

Dr. Fuller cleared her throat and drank some more coffee. They waited patiently for her to speak. Finally, she said, "We have an unusual situation with the death of Dr. Wellington. According to the local police, it's an active murder investigation. So, you need to be prepared to answer questions at any time from the police. If garden guests stop you and ask questions, please refer them to the Public Information Office inside the Visitors Center. We'll try to carry on as usual, but I'm unsure how that will look. People have a sense of macabre about these sorts of things. I suspect we'll have more than our fair share of curious visitors. And that means everything needs to be in tip-top shape."

She paused to sip coffee and continued, "Despite that, as the old saying goes, 'the show must go on.' And, we will be installing moon gardens inside and outside the conservatory. You will be working on this. Usually, all our gardens are a riot of summer color in the summer, but this year, we thought we would focus on white gardens."

"Like Sissinghurst castle!" Mari interjected.

"Yes, very much like Vita Sackville-West's vision at Sissinghurst. We'll be adding some night-blooming plants as well. In addition, we will be raising Luna Moths for release at certain events this summer." She paused and turned to Heather, "As our on-the-spot entomologist, Heather, I would like you to spearhead this. We can discuss the parameters sometime this week. For now, I have plant lists and plans for the moon gardens. This will be your task to complete by the weekend. Another part of your task is working as a team. You will be responsible for figuring out how to divide and conquer the task at hand. This is a managerial assessment."   Dr.   Fuller passed out garden plans to each of them. The group began jabbering excitedly. Mari hung back. Dr. Fuller looked at everyone again before shooing them, stating, "Go forth!"

Mari needed to talk to Detective Booker, so she approached Dr. Fuller. "Excuse me, Dr. Fuller."

"Yes, Mari. How are you doing? What can I help you with?"

"I'm doing as well as can be expected, I think. Thank you. I am eager to work on the moon gardens, but I remembered something that might be important to tell the police about Dr. Wellington's murder. May I have a few minutes to make a call to Detective Booker?"

"Of course," Dr. Fuller agreed. Mari thanked Dr. Fuller and ran to catch up with her group.

"Assign me any job," she told them, "But I have permission to make a phone call first."

Mari stepped away and went outside, pulling out Detective Booker's card and her cell phone. She dialed the number and waited anxiously for him to pick up. He did not, so she left him a message.

Mari returned to the group, relieved but frustrated, telling her teammates, "Keep me busy."They reviewed the plans with Mari, and she started removing plants and prepping the soil for the upcoming moon garden exhibit. Digging always helped her mood. She was happier with the sun shining on her and the smell of the freshly turned earth. The new plantings were exciting, and she imagined how the white flowers would look cool on hot summer days and dramatic at night. There were plans for some special, low-voltage lighting that would highlight the white blooms.

She was in her zone and didn't hear Detective Booker approach. He cleared his throat and called her name, but she didn't notice. Mari jumped, dropping her trowel, when a hand gently tapped her shoulder.

"Ms. Saille, excuse me for startling you."

Flustered, Mari brushed off her khakis and stood. She must look a sight, she thought. She knew she had dirt on her cheeks and probably in her hair. She took off the garden gloves and regained her composure.

"No problem."

"You called me and left a message. It sounded important, and since I had to return to the crime scene, I thought I would drop by to chat in person."

The other students looked at her curiously. Heather raised her eyebrows.

"Can we step outside to talk more privately?" Detective Booker requested.

"Sure," Mari agreed and told her group she would return in a few minutes.

They stepped out of the main doors of the conservatory. The morning sunshine lit the waters of the cove and the Chesapeake Bay beyond, making the wavelets sparkle like diamonds. Detective Booker looked all around, shading his eyes. He seemed to drink it all in.

"This place is rather something, isn't it?"

"Definitely," Mari said reverently. "It's a very special place."

They were caught up in Meadowood's beauty for a few minutes. She glanced at him. He was a pretty handsome guy, and she was happy he appreciated the garden's beauty.

Finally, he said, "Shall we walk a bit? What was so important to tell me?"

Mari sighed. It was the time of reckoning, "Yesterday, I inadvertently saw what I think was the murder weapon when you asked me to wait. It was like a dagger. I, uh, knew I had seen it before."

She stopped. He waited.

"This is hard for me. You see, my family, no," she hesitated, "really, my grandfather is a friend of Dr. Knight's. I think that sword is a letter opener that he had on his desk," she said miserably. "You see, he's a King Arthur fanatic. The letter opener is a replica of Excalibur. It matches the replica on the wall of his office." She paused before passionately stating, "But Dr. Knight is a good man! He would never hurt anyone! I know it!"

Detective Booker was quiet for a few minutes. They ended up in the formal French gardens, and the beautiful mansion was ahead of them.

"How well do you know Dr. Knight?" Detective Booker asked.

Mari would have squirmed in her seat, but they were walking. She twisted her hands instead. She paused before answering quietly, "I guess I really don't know him."

"I appreciate you bringing this to my attention. Otherwise, it would be withholding evidence. You did the right thing," he reassured her.

The Clock Tower chimed the quarter hour. It was nine-forty-five.

"I have class with Dr. Knight in fifteen minutes," she said miserably.

"I'll walk you back."

Detective Booker asked her about the gardens, admitting he had not visited more than a few times. Mari answered as many questions as she could. She suggested he take the tours and, perhaps, read one of the books offered in the gift shop.

"I can see why it's a special place to you. I am a history buff. Imagine living here in the nineteenth century in its heyday. I am looking forward to learning more," Detective Booker stated.

He left her at the entrance of the Visitors Center. Looking back through the glass, she saw Detective Booker phone someone. Her heart sank as she headed up to class. She felt like she betrayed Dr. Knight and couldn't look him in the eye when she slid into her seat.

The lecture was about micropropagation. Usually, Dr. Knight led interesting and interactive lectures. Today, he droned as if trying to impart as much information to them as he could quickly. He lectured on the process, how it was used in large-scale plant production, and how to keep a pest-free environment and virus-free plants. He also discussed how micropropagation was used in commercial horticulture and plant breeding. He gave some examples of plants bred exclusively at Meadowood and gave them the task of finding out which plants on the Meadowood property were bred exclusively there. That would replace a lab that afternoon and they would send him the list of found plants.

It was close to noon when two shadows appeared in the doorway. The classroom stilled, and Dr. Knight stopped his lecture. Everyone glanced at the doorway, where Detectives Parker and Booker stood silhouetted in the doorway.

"Dr. Knight, could we see you for a moment, please," Detective Parker intoned.

"Of course, sir," Dr. Knight answered, but he almost stumbled getting up and getting his cane.

Mari felt her stomach flip-flop.

"Class is dismissed. Detectives, come in. We can talk privately when the students leave."

Everyone grouped at the bottom of the stairs, whispering. Mari felt sick. Dr. Fuller came down the steps.

"What are you doing here, saplings? Off with you. I know Dr. Knight gave you an assignment. If you have any extra time, return to the moon garden project." She shooed them away, but not before she glanced up the stairs, worry written on her face.

They left. Mari hesitated. Outside, she could see through the window that the detectives were leading Dr. Knight away. Were they arresting him?

Heather came up to her. "C'mon, Mari. You can't help him."

Mari didn't think she told Heather of her personal connection to Dr. Knight, but she doubted herself.

"Why did you say that?" she asked Heather.

Heather shrugged, "I don't know. I know you like and respect Dr. Knight. I have thought it might be something more like he reminds you of your grandfather or something since he's a Brit."

Mari relaxed. She hadn't spilled the beans. "Something like that," she said faintly.

"C'mon girl, we have a lot of work to do and to catch up on from yesterday."

"Oh, right. I forgot."

"How do you want to do this? Do you want to divide and conquer?"

"Sure. That would be okay. Okay, if I start with the Woodland Gardens?"

"Yeah, and I'll take on the Meadow, Children's, and Sensory Garden."

"I want to go back to the dorm and grab a sandwich and a clipboard. Why don't I make you a sandwich?"

"Mmm, sounds like a plan. I will run into the Visitors' center and grab a couple of maps. That way, we can cross out what we did and initial."

"I want to get back to the moon garden project, too,"

Mari said. "Maybe after a couple of hours, we can plant more and check out the assigned plants in the conservatory. You go and get the maps, and I'll make lunch."

Mari walked with Heather to the northern end of the Meadowood property, carefully skirting the Clock Tower area. She could see it from every angle but didn't want to be close. Not yet, at least.

The Woodland Garden was filled with a variety of required native plantings and beautiful shade perennials. On the Woodland Garden Walk, Mari discovered many of the specialized cultivars of Meadowood. She wondered if Dr. Fuller had been integral in breeding the rare Hamamelis Ovalis. She found Meadowood cultivars of hosta, hellebores, and heuchera tucked away along the many paths. She scribbled many notes on the cultivars and located many native plants like huckleberry and poisonous algeratina altissima, or white snakeroot. She snapped photos of each and the information plaque with her phone.

Visitors seemed to overlook the Woodland Garden Walk as it was bereft of foot traffic. Many visitors went to the showier gardens, the conservatory, and the mansion rather than walking on a quiet woodland path. But there was great beauty and peace on this walk, and Mari loved it. It was just the thing she needed after the shock of finding Dr. Wellington's body. The Japanese called it forest bathing. And she found the woodlands were taking away her stress.

She was startled at hearing the sound of a flute. She continued along the path and veered off to a small grove of beech trees. Their lime-lit leaves filtered the afternoon sunlight, creating a wash of sunlight and color amongst the circle of silvery-gray trunks with bark resembling elephant skin. On a cut log sat an older man.

He was wizened, sitting slightly hunched on his perch, and could have been transported from an earlier century with his weathered khakis, cotton plaid shirt, and a vest with many pockets. His eyes were closed, and his polished wooden flute made a sweet sound. She didn't know much about music but thought it was a pentatonic scale. Its beauty made her shiver.

Mari stopped at the edge of the grove, listening. The old man must have sensed her. He opened his eyes and looked around. When he saw her, he smiled. She then recognized him. It was Boothby. He was an institution at Meadowood and somewhat of a local celebrity. He had been a gardener there all his life. Mari had seen him several times at a distance when she and her family visited. He was so dedicated that they gave him a small home at the edge of Woodland Walk, not too far from the dormitory.

"Hello," she greeted. "Your music is lovely."

He nodded his thanks. "You're welcome to sit and listen." He pointed to another stump within the grove.

Mari did so, enjoying the filtered sunshine. Boothby began to play again, and the music washed over her. She closed her eyes, remembering the Japanese term "Komorebi," which expressed the feeling of peace and awe of the feeling of the sunshine through the leaves of the trees. The music enhanced the feeling of the sunshine. She sighed audibly when his tune was finished.

"That was beautiful."

"Thank you. What brings you along this path?" asked Boothby.

Mari explained that she was a graduate student and the projects she was working on. She could talk to Boothby easily and shared her love of the garden with him. He was a kindred spirit. She did not talk about the murder but was tempted. Her phone buzzed with a text. Heather. She was late meeting her at the conservatory. Mari apologized to Boothby and left the grove, but not before he told her to stop by his house for tea sometime soon.

Feeling more settled, Mari hurried to the Conservatory. She met Heather in the Potting Shed, where they perched on stools and compared notes. Mari confessed she didn't get to the Labyrinth and told Heather about her meeting with Boothby.

Heather pulled out the plans for the Moon Gardens. Mari knew exhibits were planned over a year in advance, but she was entranced by what the garden designers put together. This was something she would love to do, to create exhibits and work with the various colors and textures of plants. Inside the conservatory doors, two identical gardens were planted with a large sea of Florida Moonlight caladium graced by small Natchez White Crape Myrtle trees on either side of the walkway. Sweet-smelling Philadelphus, or mock orange, bushes provided shiny white blossoms and a sweet scent.

There was a border of fragrant white alyssum at the edge with Diamond Frost Euphorbia, double pearl tuberoses, and large clumps of blooming white oriental lilies. Large moon flowers were set to creep up pairs of silvery trellises set with stars, created by a local artist. Crystal stars and fairy lights added to the magic. Large pots leading into the conservatory would be filled with more Florida Moonlight caladium. Outside were beds filled with white milkweed, silver artemisia, white cosmos, white butterfly bushes, candytuft, white dianthus, and white delphiniums.

"We should talk with the team about this," Mari suggested, "even though I want to jump in on the project."

"Fine," Heather admitted, "you're probably right. Let's head back to the dorm."

Everyone was in the common area surrounding the long kitchen island when they arrived.

"Have you heard?" Joe asked when they walked in the door.

"Heard what?" Heather asked, with just a note of sarcasm in her tone. "I've been up to my eyeballs in the required plant lists and the Meadowood Cultivars."

Joe ignored the sarcasm and said, "Dr. Knight has been taken in for questioning and may be charged with Wellington's murder."

"Oh, no!" Mari cried and paled visibly.

"It's not looking good," Nichelle added. "We heard a rumor that they had bad blood going back years between the two of them."

"Yeah, something about stealing research years and years ago," Ren contributed.

"And that the murder weapon was Dr. Knight's letter opener," Franklin added.

"How did you hear about this?" Heather asked.

"Oh, I listen around," Sunny said smugly. "You would be surprised at what people tell you."

"I don't think the old guy did it," Peter said. "I don't think he's the killer type."

Mari felt sick.

CHAPTER SIX

Mari not only felt sick but faint. The room seemed to swim before her eyes, and she grasped the edge of the long kitchen island. Heather noticed.

"Mari? Are you all right?"

Mari could only shake her head and murmur, "Excuse me."

She somehow made it to her room. Tears filled her eyes and blinded her momentarily. She roughly brushed them out of her eyes and fumbled with the lock on her door. Inside, she lay on the bed, curled up into a fetal position. Her stomach ached.

She felt incredibly guilty. It was her fault they had questioned Dr. Knight. *She* had told them about the letter opener. If she hadn't told them, would they have found out? Would they piece together her connection with Dr. Knight? What was the punishment for withholding information if she hadn't told them? She shivered violently with an inner chill. This was all too macabre.

There was a knock at the door.

"Come in," she called, rather faintly.

She wasn't sure she wanted to see anyone, but Heather's face peered tentatively around the door.

"Mari?" Tears threatened to spill again, and Mari waved Heather inside.

Heather entered and sat on the edge of the bed. She looked worriedly at her friend.

"Care to tell me what's going on?"

Mari nodded, but she needed to get her emotions under control. Heather spied a tumbler on Mari's desk.

"I'm going to fill this with ice water and be back in a minute."

Mari nodded, and Heather left the room. Mari hugged herself. Heather hadn't quite shut the door, and Nepeta pushed through with an inquiring meow. He jumped on the bed and bumped Mari's head and then nose. Then he licked her nose. She giggled. He plopped in next to her then, purring. Heather returned, giving the cat a look of approval. She shut the door firmly behind her.

"I brought water and a cup of hot tea. I know it's warm out, but it seemed appropriate." Heather shrugged and placed them on the bedside table.

Mari sat up and hugged her pillow, wiping her eyes again with the back of her hand. She first reached for the cold water, took a long drink, put it down, and reached for the tea, blowing on it before taking small sips.

"It's all my fault," she said quietly.

"What is?"

"Why Dr. Knight is being charged for murder." Mari looked miserably at her friend. "You see, I'm the one who told them the letter opener belonged to Dr. Knight. I recognized it." She sipped more tea.

"Mari, you can't blame yourself. Any detective would be looking for connections between the victim and the murder weapon. Anyone visiting Dr. Knight's office would have recognized that letter opener. He did display it with a lot of pride. It's part of his King Arthur 'thing,' right?"

Mari nodded.

"But, there's more, isn't there," Heather pressed.

Mari hesitated.

"No one knows this. Well, the police do now," she looked Heather in the eye, "but I don't want the information to leave this room."

Heather nodded, "Why all this cloak and dagger stuff?" she quipped.

She saw Mari's face and relented.

Mari still hesitated and, after a long pause, confessed, "My family is friends with Dr. Knight. Or rather, he's a friend with my grandad. I'm half Brit."

"So..." Heather responded.

"Don't you see how it complicates things? I feel so guilty telling the police that I recognized the letter opener. I feel as though I've betrayed not only Dr. Knight but Grandad as well."

"Give the police a little credit," Heather said acerbically. "Mari, you didn't betray anyone. If Dr. Knight is innocent, then truth will prevail. I can't see Dr. Knight killing anyone. It doesn't seem in his nature."

"I know, I know. I agree. But, all of this looks so bad for Dr. Knight." There was another long pause, and Mari asked, "What time is it?"

"Just after five."

"I need to call Grandad."

"Do you want me to leave?"

"No. Please stay here."

Mari dialed through a social media application, and moments later, her Grandad's face appeared on the screen.

"Mari, this is a lovely surprise. How are you, dear?"

Mari heard her grandmother in the background greeting her too. It was good to hear their voices. She was suddenly very homesick to see her family. She wanted a hug from someone she loved to tell her everything would be all right. Nan and Grandad were so far away.

"I'm okay," Mari started, "Actually..." She began to tear up again.

"Mari, dear, what's wrong?"

"Oh, Grandad. Everything isn't okay. I don't know how to tell you this other than to spit it out. Dr. Knight has been accused of murder!"

"What? That's absurd! Artie would never hurt a fly. What happened?"

"The other night, we had a guest lecturer here – Dr. Alexander Wellington, Esquire."

"Wellington, eh? He's a bad 'un."

"What do you mean, Grandad?"

"Artie and Wellington have been rivals for years. I'm fairly certain Wellington stole some of Artie's research. This was back in the day before computers when they all had handwritten notes and notecards. Wellington took the notes and draft of the research from Artie and published it. Artie couldn't prove that it was his. It was a huge mess. And Wellington! That guy is a pompous ass!"

"I agree, but he's dead now. I found the body."

"What?"

"Yes. It's a long story, but I found him at the base of the Clock Tower. They don't know if he was stabbed there or was stabbed in the Clock Tower and fell over the balcony. The problem is that the murder weapon looks like Dr. Knight's letter opener."

"Oh, my. That doesn't sound good. Do the police

know about the bad blood between the two men?" Grandad asked.

"I don't know, Grandad. And I know it's late, but I wanted you to know."

"Thank you, m'dear. And don't worry. It will all come out in the wash," Grandad assured her.

"I hope so. I love you, Grandad, and Nana, too."

They rang off. Heather, still seated on the bed, was wide-eyed.

"I think I need to pick up my jaw off the floor," Heather commented. "Do you still think Dr. Knight is innocent?"

Mari nodded, "I do. I can't see him killing anyone. For one thing, I don't think he's physically strong enough. Can you see him stabbing someone and pushing them off the balcony when he can't walk without that cane?"

"I'm playing Devil's advocate here," Heather added drily, "But do you think the cane is a prop? To look distinguished and all that?"

"I honestly don't know, Heather."

Mari put her head in her hands. "Oh," she moaned, "this is so confusing. But I know I want Dr. Knight exonerated. We need to help him."

"Well, I don't know about you, but this murder stuff makes me thirsty. I'm going to head down to get a couple of my beers from the fridge. Are you in?"

"I have something better than that," Mary added smugly. She pointed to a mini fridge in the corner. "I have some of my Grandad's cider."

Mari hopped off the bed and went to the mini fridge to pull out two bottles. She opened them deftly with a church key opener and handed one to Heather. Then, she clinked the bottles gently and toasted, "To Dr. Knight.

And to justice."

"Here, here," Heather added, raising her bottle. "You know, I've never had British Cider, or hard cider for that matter."

"Then you're in for a treat. This is the 'King David' varietal. It's one of my favorites because it's not too dry and it's not too sweet. It gives the depth of the flavor of the apples."

"Hark at you."

Mari shrugged. "It's the family business. I've been around ciders all my life with Grandad's Cidery. I can spout every aspect of ciders whenever you want to listen."

Heather's eyes brightened when she took a sip of the cider. She took a second and then a third to savor the flavor.

"This is delicious! And it's really complex. I don't know anything, but I like it."

"I know," Mari laughed. "Now, how can we solve this murder?"

"Well, if it wasn't Dr. Knight, then who?" "That's the question. Who would want to kill Dr. Wellington?"

"Or," Heather replied darkly, "who is trying to frame Dr. Knight? It was, after all, Dr. Knight's letter opener that killed Dr. Wellington."

"Hmm…" Mari pondered, "I can't see Dr. Fuller doing this. It would have to be someone who had a beef with one or both men, likely someone who's been to or worked with them in the UK."

"Or, the USA, or maybe on a research project somewhere else in the world."

"But, murder? What would they want to murder about?"

"Your grandad said Wellington stole Dr. Knight's

stuff. If he did it once, he would likely do it again. And I haven't gotten around to researching the Fellows program participants yet. There's been too much going on."

"You think?"

"And, maybe you can talk to the detectives again. What was his name, the detective? Detective Parker?"

Mari made a scrunchy face and pretended to gag.

"Okay then, the other one," Heather suggested, "the handsome one."

Mari blushed.

"I knew it! You like him," Heather said triumphantly, beaming at her. "What's his name?"

"Detective Booker," Mari said drily.

"That's it, Detective Booker, with the dreamy eyes."

"I think the cider is getting the best of you," Mari suggested.

"But, you'll admit, he has dreamy, liquid brown eyes with flecks of green. And, I'll agree with you, this cider has a bit of kick."

Mari blushed again. Heather hooted and raised her bottle in salute.

"I knew it."

"I'll give him a call tomorrow. I can mention the potential framing of Dr. Knight."

"And I'll research the Fellows Program tomorrow. I promise."

"That's a start. But now, let me show you what I have with the flashcards. We can add more information to the file."

"Okay, okay, back to the grindstone," Heather relented, "but finding out who the murderer is more fun."

CHAPTER
SEVEN

Mari woke the next day with determination and resolve to exonerate Dr. Knight. She couldn't imagine he was guilty of the killing of Dr. Wellington. She wondered who might want to frame Dr. Knight. But, who?

Last night, after a couple of ciders, Heather and Mari decided that she should pump Detective Booker for information, and Heather would look into the Fellows. They would divide and conquer by asking the current students and Dr. Fuller questions.

Dr. Fuller informed them that their class and lab were canceled that day. They were to continue working on the moon garden display.

Mari was stationed outside the conservatory, working with Franklin, Sunny, and Ren on the moon gardens. They had dug up the beds the previous day. Ren and Sunny got several small Philadelphus to put at the back of the gardens while Mari and Franklin planted the beautifully blooming delphiniums, tuberoses, and lilies. They were washed in the strong scent of the blooms. Mari sighed happily.

"Aren't these amazing?" she said dreamily as she tucked the plants into the soil.

"They're certainly beautiful and at peak bloom."

"So, how did you come to the program, Franklin? And, by the way, I think your name is cool. I think I read the Hardy Boys more than Nancy Drew growing up."

Franklin blushed at first and then looked slightly embarrassed. "You can thank my mom, a children's librarian, for my name. She liked the fact that our last name was Dixon and came up with the idea of honoring the book series."

"That's cool."

"I'm luckier than my brother. My dad's a history teacher. Can you guess his name?"

Mari thought quickly but shook her head, looking a little confused.

"Mason. My brother's moniker is Mason Dixon. I'm really lucky I missed that one. Give me Franklin any day."

Mari couldn't help it. She doubled over in laughter. "You're not serious, are you? Mason Dixon?" She started to giggle again.

"Cross my heart." He grinned.

"Wow. And, why Meadowood?"

"Science geek," he said perfunctorily as he plunked a tuberose into a hole he had prepared for the plant. "Specifically, trees, like Dr. Fuller. I thought about Forestry too, but I like working with the plants. I've read most of Dr. Fuller's research and wanted to study with her. You?"

"It's been a lifelong dream to work at Meadowood. I understand. I'm like you—a plant geek. I like garden design, too. These moon gardens are magical. I don't know who designed them, but I want to meet them." Mari sighed happily. She added before asking, "What do you think of the mess with Dr. Wellington and Dr. Knight?"

"I don't know what to think. Dr. Wellington came across as a pompous ass, but what do I know? Dr. Knight? I can't imagine him killing anyone. But you never know. I don't know anything about him as a person. I know more about Dr. Fuller. I hadn't heard about Dr. Wellington until that reception the other night. It's cool they are using natural compounds from the Calluna species."

Mari nodded, thinking it was a safe bet Franklin wasn't the killer."

Ren and Sunny came around the corner, taking it a little too fast in the mini truck they used to transport plants. They were whooping with laughter as they stopped in front of Franklin and Mari. The Philadelphus rocked in the back of the mini truck while Ren and Sunny were doubled over, laughing.

"What's so funny?" Franklin called as they careened to a stop and worked to control their laughter.

Ren became silent. Privately, Mari thought he was extremely moody. Her grandmother would call him an 'odd duck.'

Sunny waved her hand and answered, "Nothing! We're just being silly."

Franklin and Mari helped Ren and Sunny lift out the fragrant Philadelphus. Mari nearly swooned, taking great breaths of the highly perfumed, pearly white flowers. The citrusy scent was intoxicating, and she particularly liked the genus 'Pearls of Perfume' they were planting. Franklin and Mari had pre-dug holes for each plant, so putting them in the soil and tucking them in gently was easy.

They worked until they broke for lunch. Mari caught up with Sunny on their way back to the dorm.

"Have you caught up on your jet lag?" she asked conversationally.

"Oh, yes," Sunny informed her and added confidentially, "I only hurt myself by dosing several energy drinks, so I couldn't sleep for days. That was a big mistake. I think I'm in sync with East Coast time now."

"That's good."

"How about you? How are you doing, especially after finding Dr. Wellington's body?" She looked at Mari with sympathy. "So grisly. I'm glad it wasn't me who found him."

"So-so," Mari admitted. "I can't seem to 'unsee' the body and all that blood. The image keeps coming back and haunting me."

"I'll bet. It's too bad. Dr. Wellington seemed like an interesting guy—at least in his research. In Cali, we import so many bees to pollinate. It's cool that they've discovered something natural to help the bees. Those little buzzers keep our agricultural economy growing. I wish I knew more about that science."

"Hmm. You're right. I don't know a lot about entomology. Heather might."

Sunny cocked her head and looked at Mari, "You're right. I'll have to have a conversation with her. Maybe she'll let me help her with the Luna Moth project Dr. Fuller mentioned."

At the dorm, Sunny ran upstairs to her room. Mari rummaged in her cupboard and stared into the refrigerator for something for lunch. She would need to go to the grocery store soon. She pulled out a can of tuna, drained it, and tossed it with some salad and green olives. She added the olive brine, a little olive oil, and a few good grinds of pepper. Voila! Her favorite salad since childhood. If she had had celery, she would have chopped and added it for more crunch, but it would do for now.

Nepeta was pawing at the dormitory door. You could hear his loud, plaintive meow through the open windows. Nichelle was eating her sandwich on the couch by the door and let him in. Nepeta made a beeline to Mari and meowed at her feet for a bite of tuna.

"Thanks, Nichelle."

Nichelle smiled and nodded. She was wearing earbuds, listening to something, returning her concentration to whatever she was listening to, and eating her sandwich.

"Come upstairs with me, you mooch. I have a phone call to make."

Nepeta obediently trotted after Mari. He circled her in her room until she put some tuna on a paper towel for him to eat. She ate her salad, thinking about her conversations with Franklin and Sunny. Neither seemed to be a suspect in Dr. Wellington's death. She hoped she could talk to Ren that afternoon. She pulled out her phone to contact Detective Booker. Once again, she had to leave a message. She sighed. Nepeta came to investigate the empty bowl, and she put it on the floor for him to find a few tidbits.

Taking her bowl downstairs to clean up, she found Ren staring into the refrigerator.

"You look like I did a few minutes ago," she commented. "I know I need to go to the grocery store soon. Slim pickings in my cupboard. Not even beans for beans on toast. I have another can of tuna if you're interested," she offered.

Ren closed the refrigerator door, "Thanks, but I'm going with the old classic PB&J, although beans on toast sound rather good."

He was so formal.

"How do you know beans on toast?" she asked.

"I was born in England but spent my life in Korea. When I returned to London for college, I remembered beans on toast. It was a favorite when I was a kid. You can't beat a full English breakfast."

"That's for sure," Mari agreed, "except the vegetarian one is slightly different. I like the mushrooms and tomatoes. At least in the UK, they don't make a big deal out of vegetarianism or vegans. There are always some great options at restaurants and in the grocery stores. Here…"

Nodding in agreement, he asked, "Are you a Brit? You don't have an accent." He didn't look at her as he busied himself making his sandwich.

Mari laughed, "No, but my mom is. I have been visiting family in the UK all my life. Thus, my penchant for beans on toast."

She was going to continue, but her phone rang. It was Detective Booker.

"Excuse me," she said to Ren quickly. "I need to answer this."

Mari said hello as she went outside.

"Ms. Saille?" Detective Booker's voice came over the phone. It was a nice tenor. And, he pronounced her name correctly, saying "sigh-yeh" instead of "sail-lee."

"Call me Mari, please, Detective Booker. I wanted to share with you something my grandfather said." She hesitated before she added, "It's about Dr. Wellington."

"How can I help you, Jms. Saille?"

Mari was nervous. As they talked, she started to pace the Celtic Knot Labyrinth, winding her way through the four intertwined hearts. It was a place that always calmed her. She liked the plants that surrounded the garden. There was fragrant Spanish lavender. The fat

purple buds nodded in any breeze. In front of the lavender were mounds of silver artemisia and Grey-leaved
Euryops. They had a bright and sunny flower that con-
trasted well with the silvery gray leaves of the artemisia
and its host plant and looked bright and cheery with the
lavender. Creeping thyme bordered the edge and tried to
work its way over the bricked path.

"Well, I called Grandad because he knows Dr.
Knight. When I mentioned Dr. Wellington, he immediately responded, "He's a bad one." Grandad said Dr.
Wellington would steal other people's research findings
and publish them as his own. Grandad thought he had
more than one enemy. Grandad was certain Dr. Knight
wasn't a killer. I," she faltered, "I thought the information might be helpful."

"And, why would your Grandad know Dr. Wellington?"

She was silent for a minute and answered, "I'm not
sure. You would have to ask him."

A "hmm" came over the line, followed by a small
sigh, "Thank you, Ms. Saille. I'll add this information
to my notes."

"You're welcome, Detective."

"And, Ms. Saille," he paused, "perhaps we can talk
further this afternoon. I'll be coming back to Meadowood later today."

"All right. I am assigned to work on the new instal-
lations at the conservatory with the other students."

"I'll catch up with you then."

When they hung up, Mari realized the lunch hour
was over. She needed to hurry to the conservatory to the
team. She wondered why Detective Booker wanted to
speak with her again. And, she wanted to corner Ren,
speak with him, and compare notes with Heather."

Mari almost ran into some kids who hurtled them-selves into the labyrinth. She side-stepped quickly, almost landing in the plants. Her ankle brushed against the thyme, sending up a whoosh of scent. She glanced at the clock tower. It was getting late. She couldn't take the time to enjoy the labyrinth today and jogged the rest of the way to the conservatory, where her team was waiting for her.

"Sorry," she apologized as she returned to planting more flowers. Franklin and Ren set up solar fairy lights that they wove amongst the plantings. Sunny carefully arranged Moonflower vines on trellises. Their fat buds were ready to burst into bloom in the evening. Mari could hardly wait to see these gardens at night.

The afternoon was hot. The sun moved to the west and beat upon them as they finished the planting, water-ing, and mulching of the moon gardens. Mari felt sweat trickling down the back of her neck, and strands of hair came loose from her ponytail. She felt grubby from working on her hands and knees, putting mulch around the new plantings. They were near the end of their shift when Detective Booker came to speak with her. Her teammates nodded to her to leave with the Detective when he asked if she could spare a few minutes. Ren raised an eyebrow. It reminded her of Spock's expression in Star Trek, and she had to suppress a giggle. He smiled back. She turned her attention back to Detective Booker.

"You look parched. Do you want a drink from the café?"

"If you don't mind me looking like this." Mari waved a hand from top to toe. She was also worried she left a dirt streak when she brushed back a loose strand of hair. If she could have groaned out loud, Mari would have. She felt disgusting and wanted to run through the fountain plaza to cool off and clean off some of the dirt, but she refrained.

"You're fine," he comforted. "Lemonade?"

"Anything cool sounds terrific."

They walked around the fountain plaza toward the Visitors Center and Café. Mari looked longingly at the kids playing in the fountains. Detective Booker didn't go inside but led her to the patio that looked over Blackthorn Cove and outward to the Chesapeake Bay. It was fairly crowded, with visitors enjoying their food and the view.

"You find us a seat, and I'll get the drinks," Detective Booker offered.

Mari found a café table for two with a shady umbrella a short way away from the other Meadowood guests. She sat and looked out at the stilled blue water of Blackthorn Cove. Even the water seemed hot today, and made little effort to send small waves to shore. Detective Booker returned with two sweating glasses filled with ice and lemonade. Mari wished she could jump into the cool glass head first. She told him thank you and forced herself to sip the icy, sweet-sour liquid slowly.

Detective Booker let her sip her lemonade for a minute. He seemed to stare at the horizon where the water met the sky. From this viewpoint, you could barely see the land on the other side of the bay. It looked like a thin, squiggly line from a graphite pencil.

She studied him, admiring his quiet way of appraising things around him. And he turned those liquid brown eyes with green flecks on her; she felt her stomach flip. She chided herself to focus.

He cleared his throat before saying, "Ms. Saille, you seem to have some personal character information about Dr. Knight from your grandfather?"

"Yes."

"And…"

"Grandad said that Dr. Wellington had many people upset with him. He said, "he's a bad one." And I was thinking other people at Meadowood might have a connection with Dr. Wellington. Dr. Knight isn't the only Brit here. And, with Dr. Wellington's reputation of where he's lectured, I'm sure some of the students and fellows, and probably other gardeners have had a chance to run into him in the last few years. I can't see Dr. Knight hurting a fly, let alone murder someone."

"Have you been playing Nancy Drew?"

She sat up suddenly and stammered, "N-n-no, not exactly."

"Leave this to the police, please. There's a murderer out there, Ms. Saille. They struck once. They may strike again."

"But…"

"No 'buts.' Leave the murder investigation alone. And, Dr. Knight hasn't been charged," he paused, "yet. There's evidence…" and he stopped.

Mari looked at him questioningly, but he was quiet. He wasn't going to say anything else. She quietly responded, "Yes, sir," quelled at the thought of the murderer running loose.

"Good," he stated firmly. "But, I would also like to speak with your grandfather. Do you have his number?"

"Yes, I do." She fished her phone out of her pocket, "But, please remember they're five hours ahead. If you call now, he may be getting ready for bed. He's Dr. Knight's age, and he and Nan turn in early."

"I'll do my best to remember," he assured her and smiled.

"Oh, okay. Thank you again for the lemonade."

"You're very welcome." He smiled at her, and her

stomach flipped again very nicely.

After Detective Booker left, Mari started for the dorm. She wanted to talk to Heather and shower. On her walk back to the dormitory, she texted Heather but didn't receive a response. The common area was empty except for Peter, who poked around the refrigerator. She greeted him, ran to Heather's room, and banged on the door.

"Hey! What's going on?" Heather demanded at the loud pounding. Seeing Mari, she said, "Oh! Come in!"

Heather had been in the shower and wrapped her hair in a towel. The bathroom light was still on. It was slightly steamy in her room, and Mari smelled fresh soap and shampoo. Heather's room looked out at the Woodland Garden. She had been correct in telling Mari it was like a treehouse. Pale green curtains with tree silhouettes graced the windows, giving the room an ethereal feel. Heather had piles of books strewn everywhere. Her bedspread was a colorful quilt with a huge dragonfly. It was bunched up and Mari could see forest green sheets printed with flying insects. A stuffed tardigrade pillow was near the top of the bed, perched like a teddy bear. Mari couldn't help but smile knowing her friend's love of six-legged critters and everything that crawled and flew.

"What's up?"

"Detective Booker. He bought me a lemonade and told me to keep my nose out of the murder case."

"Woo-hoo!" Heather teased, "A date!"

"Silly," Mari shook her head. "I look like a mud wren. I'm a mess. He wanted to make sure he told me to mind my business and stop playing Nancy Drew."

"Still…" Heather argued, "he didn't have to come all the way to Meadowood to tell you that. He could have told you that on the phone."

Mari rolled her eyes at her friend and changed the

subject, "Look, I'm almost out of food. Do you want to do some grocery shopping tonight? I need to shower first, though."

"Sure. Maybe we can grab a slice of pizza or something before we hit the store and buy it out."

"Sounds like a plan. And there's a sub shop near the grocery store with vegan meats," she tempted Heather, waggling her eyebrows.

"Even better!"

"Give me twenty minutes."

Mari hurried back to her room, petted Nepeta quickly, and jumped into the shower. She scrubbed her head with the shampoo and thought more about her conversation with Detective Booker. Granted, he was looking out for her, but she was helping him and Dr. Knight. She wondered if he would follow through and call Grandad. She would need to call him tomorrow and find out.

Feeling much better after a shower, Mari met Heather in the common room. Mari was starving and offered to drive. They climbed into her older, blue compact car. Mari turned on the air conditioning immediately.

"What did you find out today?"

Heather screwed up her face and whined, "I didn't have much time—just lunch. I looked up the Fellows on the Meadowood website. Felicity Kent is British. She's a possibility. Not sure about the others unless they met Dr. Wellington at a conference or took a class with him. The others are from Brazil, Belgium, and the USA."

"Hmm…" Mari answered, "And Ren is British by birth. He spent his life in Korea and returned to London for college. Franklin and Sunny don't seem like prospects for being murderers."

"I'm glad of that," Heather said drily. "I spoke with Nichelle. She's great, and she isn't a murderer.

That woman eats, breathes, and drinks flowers. That's her main focus in life. And did you know that Peter's a mycologist? That's his focus."

Mari shook her head.

She drove to the northern edge of town, past the police station and the library. She pulled into the plaza with the grocery store and the sandwich shop. They went in, ordered their food, and found a small booth.

"Now, tell me more about these Fellows."

Heather shrugged, "I'm sorry, I don't have more information. As I mentioned earlier, the Felicity woman might be someone of interest. She's a Brit. She lost her job as a professor when they moved funding. She had to switch careers and become a landscape designer."

"Wow. Was Dr. Wellington involved?"

"I don't know yet. But the police should probably look into it. Dr. Wellington sounds like a horrible man. Speaking of..." she had glanced up and now looked pointedly at Mari.

"What?" Mari asked, craning around.

She paled a little, seeing Detective Parker enter the sandwich shop to pick up a 'to-go' order. He saw them.

"Well, well, well. If it isn't Nancy Drew and her companion," he said with a nasty edge. "You need to leave the policing to the police, young lady," he pointedly said to Mari.

"Yes, sir. I understand," Mari told him, her eyes wide.

She may have looked innocent to him, but inside, she was fuming. How dare he!

They were interrupted by the arrival of their sandwiches.

"Bon Appetit," Detective Parker said in a sarcastic tone.

He left the sandwich shop. Mari thought Heather would explode. Her dark, auburn curls seemed to crackle with her anger.

"What a horrible man!" she exploded with a loud whisper. "Nancy Drew indeed! It makes me want to go and solve this murder just to stick it to him."

"I know what you mean. And Detective Booker warned me, too. He said I need to be careful because the killer is still running around." She paused, "Wait! He must also think Dr. Knight is innocent if he said that! And, he was about to say something else but stopped."

"Could be," Heather agreed, biting into her sandwich. "Hey, this is really good. I'm glad you know the local spots. I'm a stranger in a strange land in Maryland. I'm from the hinterlands of New England."

"Where you spent a lot of time looking at bugs," Mari added with a laugh.

"You got that right." Heather sighed. "Halcyon days."

Mari could imagine her friend lying on the ground to watch ants or chasing after butterflies and dragonflies.

"What about the rest of our team? I hate to think anyone would be a murderer," Mari shuddered at the thought.

"Well," Heather said, taking a long drink from her soda, "like I said earlier, Nichelle is all about flowers. There isn't a violent bone in her body. I'm convinced of that. Peter?"

"Maybe he had one too many magic mushrooms. Maybe that's why he's so laid back."

"But, is he? Really? We don't know a lot about him."

"Speaking of not knowing about people, what about Joe? He was arguing with Dr. Knight a couple of days ago. Right before Dr. Wellington's talk. What about him? And how can I leak that piece of information to Detective Booker without sounding like Nancy Drew? I am so frustrated!"

"Joe's a mystery for sure," Heather agreed. "I didn't get a chance to talk to him much. One of us will need to corner him. And, Dr. Fuller?"

"We don't know a lot about her, but Franklin does. She's the reason he's here. He wants to study under her."

"She always seems, I don't know, like she's suppressing something. Anger? Frustration? I don't know."

"So, we need to learn more about the Fellows, Peter, Joe, and Dr. Fuller, right?"

"And, who killed Dr. Wellington?"

CHAPTER EIGHT

Still tousled from sleep, Mari called her grandfather the next morning.

"Hello, Luv," her grandfather greeted her.

"Hi, Grandad. How are you?"

"We can't complain. Your Nan is already in the garden attacking the weeds."

"I can see her doing that. She's pretty fierce about keeping the garden weed-free. Meadowood would hire her in an instant," she joked.

"You're right about that," he chuckled. "By the way, a detective called me yesterday."

"Hmm, I was wondering. That's why I called."

"Nice young man," Grandad complimented. "I told him what I could. He also mentioned he wants you to stay out of police business."

"I am, Grandad, honest! Geez, I was trying to help Dr. Knight. He didn't kill anyone."

"I know Artie wouldn't kill anyone, but they have to prove it. Apparently, he met with Wellington after the lecture."

"How do you know?"

"That detective of yours let it slip."

"He's not *my* detective."

"Right-o. He let it slip that Artie's cane made some indentations around the clock tower where Wellington was stabbed."

"Could Dr. Knight even get up the Clock Tower stairs? I mean, it looked like Wellington took a nose-dive from the balcony. He was," she hesitated and took a breath, seeing the body in her mind, "He was all crumpled, like a rag doll. And the blood…" she added faintly.

"Now, Marigold, put that out of your mind," her grandfather ordered.

"I keep trying," she responded, sighing. "It's hard."

"Death, by any means, isn't a pretty sight. But it's a reality. It certainly comes closer to me every day."

"Grandad! No!"

"Well, I am getting older, dear. But murder is a different story. It's ugly, violent, and senseless. And we both know Artie is innocent. Why the man lives half in his garden world, and the other half, he's mooning about King Arthur. You should hear him after a few ciders. My God! Can that man wax on about King Arthur! Did you know he's mapped all the places Arthur may have been in Britain? And he's visited all the sites. He should have gone into history instead of botany, but like Wellington, he's got a soft spot for heaths and heathers – and his beloved Scottish and Welsh hills. When a blight hit many years ago, he was like Lancelot and the other Knights to save the heathers. It turned out it was some root rot from a fungus. But I digress even more, other than the pesky murder situation, are you happy at Meadowood, Mari?"

"Oh, Grandad, it's my dream. I love learning and

working here. I want to learn more about garden design. We just installed these cool moon gardens for a summer display inside and outside the Conservatory. They're stunning! You know, my professor, Dr. Fuller, calls us saplings in a nice sort of way. I feel like a sapling that's been planted in the Woodland Walk. I want to stretch my roots and my branches and grow, grow, grow. I sort of want to be like Boothby."

"Who?" her Grandad interrupted.

"Boothby. He's an old gardener who's been at Meadowood forever. He's been here so long that they built him a cottage. It's close to the dormitory. I met him officially the other day while checking out the required plants on the Woodland Walk. He was playing a gorgeous Native American wooden flute. But that's a story for another day. I need to get ready, and fast. Dr. Fuller is a stickler about being on time."

Her grandfather laughed. "Go and get ready, dear heart. It was lovely talking with you. I am so glad Artie has someone in his corner, the old coot. I miss both of you."

"Thanks, Grandad. Love to Nan and love you too."

She rang off. Moments later, she was in the kitchen.

"You're late," Heather warned as she flew into the room. "Everyone else has gone ahead."

"I know. I know. I was talking with Grandad. Thanks for waiting for me, Heather."

Mari grabbed a banana, opened it, and slathered it with almond butter. "Let's go!"

They hurried out the door to the Potting Shed. They entered as the Clock Tower chimed. Dr. Fuller's eyebrows were raised as far as they could, but she didn't say anything. She took another sip of her coffee and closed her eyes reverently for a moment.

"All righty, then," she announced. "Before more rumor swirls, they are holding Dr. Knight. He has not been charged as yet. Your plant propagation classes are on hold until we resolve this mess around Dr. Wellington and they find the murderer. I'm talking with the Meadowood officials about starting my tree class, but they've asked me to wait a few more days. Until things are resolved, we'll use your assistance around the garden. You'll be assigned to different areas for the mornings. After your lunch break, you are to study the required plant lists. Know them inside, outside, backward, and forward. There will be no excuses for the exam because you have extra time to learn the plants." She gave them each a hard look before continuing. "The afternoons are not 'off' or time to laze around. You are to be focusing on the required plant list. Understood?"

Dr. Fuller waited until everyone nodded in agreement.

"I've prepared a schedule."

She waved a sheaf of papers at them. "Let me know if you have any questions."

The schedules were distributed. Mari was delighted to see she was assigned to the Conservatory this week. Nichelle had been assigned to the Flower Garden Walk, and Franklin and Peter were assigned to the Woodland Garden area. Sunny, known by the happy squeals from her direction, was assigned to the Herb and Physick Gardens. She didn't see Heather's name anywhere except for a 'see me' by her name. Joe and Ren were assigned to the formal gardens. Most of them, Mari realized, were in areas that they loved. It was a nice gesture, considering the turmoil of the week.

Mari wondered about her job. What would she be doing in the Conservatory? As if reading her mind, Dr. Fuller called her over.

"Mari, take this bucket and this grabber stick, and you'll be going section by section and dead-heading the plants in all the displays. Everything needs to be at peak bloom for the visitors. If you see something awry, if a plant or plants are not doing well, it's your job to let me know as soon as possible. Since you're the sole student assigned to the Conservatory, I suggest you focus on one or two areas each day. You'll see volunteers and docents around. Talk to them. Learn as much as you can about the Conservatory and its plants." She paused and then addressed the group, "And I neglected to mention that you should journal your experiences in each garden each day, along with plant discussion. This is to be submitted to me daily. Understood?"

"Yes, Dr. Fuller," chorused from the students' mouths.

Someone groaned quietly, but Mari didn't see who it was.

"Scoot, saplings. Get tools, go to your assigned areas, and begin to work. Contact me if you have any questions. I'll be in my office—Mari, head upstairs. Heather, you come with me. They were dismissed.

Mari was quite happy to be working in the Conservatory. She wasn't quite puttering around the garden rooms, but almost. She dead-headed and carefully picked up stray leaves and blossoms. She reveled in the plants' colors, textures, and arrangements of each display. She looked up and around the Conservatory in awe. Lord Blackthorn had the Conservatory built just after the Civil War. Rumor, was he hired former soldiers to give them work. It was stunning. It was a smaller version of the Crystal Palace and looked a little like the Phipps Conservatory in Pittsburgh, although that was built much later. It was stunning architecture. She knew the Meadowood

Foundation worked tirelessly to update the building and preserve its historical integrity. She continued to meander through the Conservatory, taking photos of required plants and their informational plaques for her flashcard project. She would need to update Dr. Fuller on what she was doing. And she would need to call her brother for some pointers on printing the flashcards.

As if on cue, Dr. Fuller approached her. "Ms. Saille, it's lunchtime. But I also need to speak with you for a moment. I know you have had a stressful week, but you must keep up with your work."

"Yes, ma'am," Mari answered. "I'm working to convert the list of required plants into flashcards. I should be able to finish by tomorrow and then figure out how to print them."

"Flashcards, eh? That's a good idea. I will be interested in your final product. Send me what you have this evening to see how far you have progressed. When do you think you'll have the flashcards available?"

"Probably sometime next week. I was going to ask my brother to have them printed and sent here. I'm not sure yet. I don't know of an office supply store in this area."

Dr. Fuller raised her eyebrows. "Office supply store? No, you would find a feed or hardware store easier than an office supply store." She paused and looked around, "You're doing a fine job here. Go take a break, and then continue in here this afternoon. I'm hoping things will return to normal, whatever that is."

"Thank you, Dr. Fuller. I'll send you what I have completed."

Dr. Fuller nodded and took a sip from her ever-present coffee cup. She looked around, stating, "I need to come here more often. It's peaceful, like the forest."

She said it more to herself than Mari, so Mari just nodded, unsure if the professor had seen it. Dr. Fuller wandered away, coffee in one hand and a hand outstretched to gently brush the plants. Mari understood and put her things away in the potting shed before returning to the dorm.

It was quite late in the lunch hour when she walked into the common area. It was bereft of students other than Joe, and she was a little surprised to see him there. She didn't interact much with him and felt like she hadn't talked to him in days.

"Hi, Joe," she greeted.

"Hi," he returned, a dour note in his voice.

Mari wondered if Heather had talked to him. A sour-faced man replaced the happy-go-lucky guy.

"Everything okay?" she ventured, asking tentatively.

Joe sighed, "I guess. Nothing I want to discuss, okay?"

He looked at her, and she noticed his eyes were colder than usual.

"Sure, no worries. I'm running really late and need to grab something to eat. Dr. Fuller came to the Conservatory to scold me for not turning in my stuff. It's been a little crazy with Dr. Wellington's murder and the constant questions from the police."

She felt like she was babbling and went over to her cupboard to pull out a couple of slices of bread. Mari put them in the toaster. She turned to face Joe, who was gathering his things.

"It's all work, work, work around here," Joe agreed. "I need to get back."

"See you later," she said to his retreating back.

Wow, she thought. To think he was tossing a football a couple of days ago. I wonder what happened? And he was arguing with Dr. Knight. I wonder what that was all about. I'll need to check with Heather to see if she talked to him. He's a puzzle.

Her toast popped up, and she filled her sandwich with olive hummus, tomatoes, and a little onion and went to sit outside in the sun on a bench near their front door. She turned her face to the warm spring sun. She glanced at the time. She needed her notebook to work on the plant lists and texted Heather about what they needed to add to their list. Since she spilled the beans on the flashcard idea, she would need to work late on completing the file. And she would need to call her brother.

Her phone beeped. Heather was already out in the gardens working on the lists. She asked Mari to finish the lists from the Conservatory and the Labyrinth. Heather was finishing the lists in the Physick and Herb gardens and the area around the mansion. She asked if Mari could meet up later to pull the list together. Mari texted a 'thumbs up' emoji back.

She finished her portion of the project fairly quickly. Feeling accomplished, she texted Heather an update and returned to the dormitory. Nepeta was waiting for her by the dormitory door, stretched out fully in the sunshine. He blinked at her when she approached, yawned, stretched, and stood up to rub against her legs.

"Hello, Nepeta," Mari greeted him, stroking the sun-warmed cat from head to tail. "Do you want to come inside with me?"

Nepeta responded with a meow and walked over for Mari to open the door.

"I have work to do," she warned the cat as he followed her upstairs.

Mari opened the door to her room, and Nepeta raced for the patch of sunshine on the window seat.

"Look at you," she told the cat, "Taking the best seat in the house. I suppose your work is to keep that spot warm."

Nepeta ignored her and proceeded to lick his paw and groom himself. Mari went to the desk and, tongue between her teeth, opened the file for the flash cards. She lost track of time uploading photos and information. Heather knocked on her door and let herself into Mari's room.

"Hey there."

"Hi," Mari greeted, raising her arms and stretching from side to side.

"I sent the other files."

"Great! I'll take a little break, finish this, and send it to Dr. Fuller. I don't think that I texted you that she stopped by the Conservatory today and scolded me to get this project completed."

"Yeah, she scolded me too when I went to her office to discuss the Luna Moth thing." Heather scratched at her head. "I don't think it's a feasible project. A butterfly house would be a better idea. Luna Moths only live for a week. They don't eat. I don't think the garden guests want to see caterpillars all over the place. She seemed satisfied when I told her I would work on an educational piece."

"When are you supposed to do that?" Mari asked.

Heather shrugged. "I guess I won't sleep much in the next few weeks. It will be okay. I like planning this kind of stuff. And, by the way, she's worried about you."

"Me? Why?"

"Because you found the body and stuff. She seemed to know that you had a connection to Dr. Knight without saying so."

"Hmm..." and Mari changed the subject. "Have you

had a chance to talk with Joe?"

"Nope. He's never around."

"I saw him at the tail end of lunch today. He was in a really bad mood."

"Joe? He's usually like a puppy, all playful and happy."

"I know. He definitely didn't want to talk to me."

"Well, I'm stumped."

"Me too," Mari said with a sigh. "And poor Dr. Knight is still in jail."

"I think they need to either charge him or let him go. It's something like forty-eight or seventy-two hours you can be held before being charged."

"How do you know that?"

"Television. True crime. And I had a pre-law roommate in college who talked in her sleep. I can tell you, I learned a lot."

"So, it's been two days. I wonder…"

"Look, don't wonder too much. I'll make us dinner if you can finish the flashcards."

"And I need to talk to someone in my family to take the file to the office store for printing and laminating before either bringing it here or sending them to us. Dr. Fuller seemed interested in the flashcards."

"She should. It's a fantastic idea, Mari. You'll be getting brownie points for sure. They may even take the file and get it reproduced for us and future students."

Mari blushed. "Go cook," she told Heather, a little embarrassed. "It's been mostly fun."

Heather left to head to the kitchen, and Mari returned to the project. She imported Heather's information, tweaked it, and finished. She clapped her hands in triumph before sending the large file to Dr. Fuller. She sent a copy to Heather. Next, she looked up office supply businesses that would print and send the flashcards.

She grimaced at the price. She glanced at her printer. It would likely take most of her ink, but she really wanted a prototype. With another grimace, she pressed print and watched the cards start spitting out of the printer.

While they were printing, she emailed her mom and dad to please send her toner and paper as soon as possible, explaining her project. There was a bang at the door, and Mari went to open it. Heather stood with two steaming bowls, something that smelled fantastic.

"I thought we could use some comfort food. It's a mushroom gravy over rice." She glanced over at the printer, whirring along and printing. "You're finished?"

"Yup. And the file is sent to Dr. Fuller, and you, of course."

"Fantastic! Thank you!"

"You're welcome. I also looked up office supply stores that can print and send us the cards. It's a little expensive, though."

"Let's cut and fold these after we eat and show them to Dr. Fuller. Maybe Meadowood will spring for the printing. You never know…"

"Good idea."

CHAPTER NINE

Mari yawned and hit the snooze on her alarm twice before getting up. She and Heather spent most of the previous evening cutting, folding, and gluing the flashcards together. She tied them in a pretty ribbon and was eager to share them with Dr. Fuller.

She wondered what this day would bring. A small knot of tension formed in her stomach when she realized it was Dr. Knight's third day in jail. She wondered if they would let him go or charge him with the murder of Dr. Wellington. Worriedly, she hugged Nepeta, who had been sound asleep. He squirmed in her arms, then settled and began to purr.

She was glad she would be returning to the Conservatory this morning. She put the flashcards and sunblock in her small backpack and went downstairs. It was a beans-on-toast sort of day and comfort food for her.

"Hey, Ren," she called to him when he entered the kitchen. "I have extra. Do you want some beans on toast?"

He gave her a bright smile and nodded. "Thanks! I have some Yorkshire tea if you would like some."

"Would I ever!" Mari said excitedly. "That's what my Grandad and Nan drink. What a treat."

"I'm assuming you want cream and sugar?"

"Yes, sir!"

They sat at the table with their small, British breakfast.

"Now, if we only had the full English to go with this," Ren mourned.

"You can have the bacon and stuff, but I would happily take the tomato and fried mushrooms, but I do like some of the Vegan haggis you can get in the UK," Mari told him. "Thanks for the tea."

"Thanks for the beans on toast. Look, I'll wash up since you made breakfast."

"Thanks, Ren. I need to roust Nepeta and put him outside."

"That cat is spoiled."

"Absolutely."

She ran back to her room to get her backpack and to pick up a protesting Nepeta.

"C'mon, kitty-cat. You get to go to work, too," she told him while carrying him outside.

He stalked away from her, head high and tail switching. He wasn't happy. Mari hurried to the potting shed to arrive first. Dr. Fuller was there sipping her coffee. She raised her eyebrows when Mari came in, somewhat breathless.

"I sent the file to you last night, but I wanted you to see a prototype of the flashcards," she told her professor. "This was a joint project for Heather and me, with the murder and all."

"I saw the file. Very impressive work, Mari. Thank you for the prototype. I will see if we can get these printed and laminated for your lot. Well done."

Mari blushed. The other students drifted in. Dr. Fuller sipped her coffee and waited for everyone to gather. When everyone arrived, she cleared her throat.

"This morning, you will be assigned to the same portions of the garden as yesterday. We'll have a class this morning, promptly at ten. I've heard some grumbles about the required plant list project. I will, at ten, go over several reasons why you completed this assignment. Also, there's been a change in plans for this afternoon. With the murder business of Dr. Wellington, we have been remiss in getting the graduate students and the Fellows together for a meet and greet. We'll do this this afternoon with a casual luncheon at one. We will once again be at the mansion. Please, be prompt."

Everyone continued to wait for Dr. Fuller to continue. She sipped her coffee and, as usual, closed her eyes reverently. When she opened them, she saw them still standing there.

"You are dismissed, scions. Shoo! I will see you at ten in the classroom area." She waved them off.

Mari was happy to return to the Conservatory. This morning, she would check the main area quickly but move on to the Rainforest Garden and the Mediterranean Room. Each garden had a distinctive feel. She loved the colorful blooms in the Mediterranean Room. Various lavenders and rosemary plants graced the rocky ground along with spurge, Santolina, and colorful Bougainvillea. This garden had lovely scents, and she breathed deeply. There were quiet, bubbling fountains in tall cobalt blue urns placed artfully among the plants. This was a calm space. She found herself relaxing and picking spent blooms and trimming. The bubbling of the fountains lulled her. That is until her phone alarm jolted her back to reality. The two hours in the Conservatory had passed quickly, and it was time to clean up and get to the classroom. Mari hurried and scurried, meeting Heather on the sidewalk to the Visitors Center.

"How has your morning been?" Heather asked.

"I love working in the Conservatory," Mari told her dreamily. "I can't decide which garden room is my favorite. I love them all."

"You are so silly," Heather teased. "You are a garden maniac."

"Absolutely, and proud of it," Mari replied.

They laughed together as they entered the classroom and joined the others.

"As I mentioned earlier," Dr. Fuller began, "I've heard the comments of discontent about the required plant lists. Some of you may think this is busy work, but I can assure you it is not. A term was used several years ago called "Plant Blindness." It refers to how people overlook plants even though they are essential to our environment. As future leaders in the plant world and the Botanic Garden world, it's essential that you are aware of plants. You need to recognize plants as an important part of our world; you need to classify them not only as something visually beautiful but also categorize them as living organisms. You need to have a foundation of knowledge of the plants. You are not only stewards to the Botanical Gardens you'll be working in but also to our Earth. You need to bring plant awareness to visitors to the gardens. So, your so-called," she paused and made air quotes, "busy work" with the required plant list isn't busy work at all. It's an introduction to some of our plant collections at Meadowood and a fairly typical foundation list of plants in the North American setting."

Dr. Fuller went on to describe the different plant

collections at Meadowood. Mari took notes as rapidly as possible. Somehow, she knew the information would end up on an exam. Finally, Dr. Fuller ended her lecture. She glanced at Heather, who looked at her and shook her wrist. Mari nodded in agreement.

"One last thing, before we break, prepare for our luncheon and 'Meet and Greet' with the Fellows --two of you did an exceptional job on the required plant list. These two students have made your learning much easier."

Mari's head shot up. She looked quickly at Heather and then back at Dr. Fuller.

"Marigold Saille and Heather Arum created flashcards of the required plants. The powers at Meadowood have provided funding to print and laminate the flashcards for each of you. So, thank you, Mari and Heather. Well done."

"If this were Harry Potter, you would have won points for your house," Franklin quipped so quietly that only Mari heard. He was sitting directly behind her and leaned forward. She glanced back at him, and he hid a chuckle. She couldn't help but smile.

"Now, shoo, scions. I'll see you in an hour at the mansion."

They filed out of the room. Sunny caught up with Mari and Heather and put an arm through each girl's elbows.

"You two are amazing! I am indebted to you for making those flashcards. What a great idea."

"I'll say," Nichelle piped up, coming up behind them. "They'll save us mounds of time. I can't believe Meadowood is going to print them for us."

"It's very nice of them," Mari agreed. "I put them together because I thought it would be a great way to learn the plants."

"I wonder when the exam will be?"

"Who knows? Things are a mess with what's happened with Dr. Wellington and Dr. Knight. I'm sure the administration and the Foundation are scrambling to make things hunky-dory before it goes crazy in the press and social media," Sunny contributed.

Mari wanted to change the subject, "Have you met any of the Fellows?" she asked the group.

"I have," Sunny piped up. "That nice Armand, from Belgium. I was talking with him at Dr. Wellington's lecture. He's cool. He does moveable sculptures in gardens worldwide, but he's based in Belgium."

"I met the US Fellow Rebecca Collins. She's terrific. She is an expert on Florida's botany. She worked at this park. I can't remember the name, but it was a cult in the early 20th century. I spoke to her more about the plants in Florida than the cult," Nichelle said.

"And there's someone from England, right?"

"And Brazil," Heather piped in, picking up on Mari.

"I guess we'll meet them sooner than later," Sunny said. "I want to freshen up. Meet you in the common room in twenty minutes?"

Everyone agreed. Mari went to her room to freshen up and put on a clean, dirt-smudge-free Meadowood shirt. She wasn't sure if they were permitted to wear street clothes to this event. And, who knew, Dr. Fuller might send them back to work in the gardens. She wanted to meet and talk with the British Fellow to see if there was a connection between them and Dr. Wellington or Dr. Knight. Time was running out for Dr. Knight. She was worried they would charge him for murder, and she knew, deep down, that he wasn't guilty. Dr. Knight was one of those people who were like a light in the darkness. She returned to the common area, where she met the group to walk to the mansion.

As with the reception a few days ago, the café chefs had outdone themselves. There was a spectacular spread of delicious food. Dr. Fuller met them at the door.

"Mingle," she stage whispered. "Get your lunch and talk to someone you've never met."

Mari and Heather walked to the table. They were both pleased to see chickpeas stuffed into a pita with vegetables. It was labeled 'spicy falafel,' and they took it eagerly. They filled their plates with other nibbles and salads. Dr. Fuller caught Mari's eye. She put two fingers together and had them move apart. She pointed at Mari and Heather and repeated the gesture.

"Uh, Heather? Dr. Fuller wants us to split up."

Heather turned to Mari and rolled her eyes out of Dr. Fuller's sight. "Really? Okay, here we go."

Heather approached a woman with dark brown hair and sparkling blue eyes. "Hello," Mari heard her say. I'm Heather Arum, a graduate student. And you?"

Mari didn't hear the woman's response but looked around. A petite blond woman was near the fireplace and the dessert table. She looked as though she was considering her dessert choices. Mari sidled up to her.

"They look good, don't they? I can personally recommend the Snowberry Cream with the Raspberry Coulis. It's one of my favorites."

The woman turned to look at her. "Really? I love raspberries. I'll give it a try."

"The chocolate mousse and the passionfruit tart are amazing too."

"How do you know all the desserts they're offering?"

The woman's voice was British, with a posh, British accent. This must be the Fellow from the UK.

Mari laughed, "My family and I have been coming

to Meadowood all my life. And now, it's pretty dangerous to be living on the café's doorstep with these decadent desserts. I'm Mari, by the way, one of the graduate students."

"I'm Felicity. Felicity Kent, one of the Fellows."

"Where are you from in the UK? I can't quite place it. My Granddad and Nan live on the Scottish borders."

"Yorkshire originally, but schooled in London," Felicity answered. "Graduate student, eh? You're just starting your career. What's your focus?"

"I'm not sure yet," Mari answered honestly, "but garden design is at the top of my list. I'm eager to learn more."

"Well, I might be able to help you with that," Felicity told her, "Garden design is one of my specialties. And, I have to help a fellow countryman – or half-countryman, so to speak."

"Thank you," Mari replied graciously. "I would love to talk with you further. We're not the only Brits here, you know. Ren," she nodded at the young man talking with a gentleman in a black polo shirt, "was born in London and raised in Korea. He returned to London for college. And, of course, there's Dr. Knight. And, poor, unfortunate Dr. Wellington."

Mari felt like she was babbling but wanted to observe this woman's reactions when she brought up the names. Felicity Kent seemed to flinch between the mention of Dr. Knight and Dr. Wellington. Or was it her imagination? She wondered quickly how she could ask if she knew them. She assumed she could spit it out. Honesty worked, right?

She was about to ask when Dr. Fuller clanged on a glass with a spoon to get their attention. When everyone had quieted, she said, "I'm so glad you were able to come to this meet and greet today. Thank you to the café and their staff," she nodded to the workers in green aprons stationed around the room, "for this fabulous food. As you know, it's been an odd week with Dr. Wellington's demise, and I'm afraid that Dr. Knight…"

The door opened, and Dr. Knight entered, "Has arrived, late as usual. I hope you left me a bite or two."

"Dr. Knight! You're back!" Dr. Fuller was gaping like a fish.

"Guilty as charged," he quipped, "Although not for murder, just to return to my post."

You could have heard a pin drop. Mari looked around the room. Many faces eager to see Dr. Knight were smiling. Dr. Fuller looked shocked. Ren looked bored and moody. Joe looked stormy. Felicity stood stock still, her face frozen in a mask. Her genuine smile of a moment ago was gone and replaced with a fake smile.

Mari thought, 'This *is a fine kettle of fish*,' borrowing one of her Nan's favorite expressions. Three people seemed bothered by Dr. Knight's return. Did one of these three kill Dr. Wellington, or were they looking to frame Dr. Knight? She couldn't wait to talk to Heather.

Dr. Fuller recovered and stopped gaping at Dr. Knight's unexpected appearance.

"Dr. Knight! Huzzah! Welcome back!" Dr. Fuller cried, applauding him.

Everyone else followed suit, and there was a smattering of light applause.

"Thank you, thank you, everyone. It's good to be home."

"Excuse me," Felicity told Mari. "I enjoyed our conversation but need to talk later."

Felicity left Mari's side and approached Dr. Knight with a bright, false smile, saying, "Artie! You beat the rap! Isn't that what they say in America?"

Dr. Knight laughed and nodded. They walked to another corner of the room where they could chat privately. It was good to know Felicity Kent knew Dr. Knight so well. Mari raised her eyebrows.

Dr. Fuller raised her voice so that all could hear, "Let's get back to our little soiree, everyone. Thank you."

She turned to get more food and almost walked into a tall, dark-haired gentleman.

"Hello," he greeted her in accented English. "I am Anastacio Santos, the Fellow from Brazil. And you are?"

"Marigold, that is Mari Saille, graduate student," she said shyly to the charismatic man before her. His deep voice sent ripples through her. Then, bravely, she asked, "What brought you to Meadowood?"

He shrugged casually, "I am working on my doctorate and thought it was a good opportunity. I took the time off from my graduate degree at Penn State."

"Penn State?" Mari queried, "That's in Central Pennsylvania, right?"

"Right," he agreed, "beautiful country in the blue mountains. I believe they refer to them as mothers' mountains as they are beautifully rounded."

He made a gesture and Mari wasn't sure if he meant what she thought, and blushed.

"And, what's your focus?" she asked him.

"Ahh, I hope to return to my native land to teach, of course, but also go into the jungles to look for new plant species." He grinned, "a little like Indiana Jones looking for treasure. There are miles of unexplored rain forest in Brazil."

"But, a dangerous proposition?" Mari asked.

He nodded, "It can be. But, right now, I'm playing it safe and working with palm trees. Palm oil is extremely lucrative, but as with many things, we need to make the farms more sustainable."

"Interesting," Mari commented. "And, what's the Fellows program like?"

He sighed, "It is another notch on my resume. We will have many discussions, refine our skills, and speak with garden leaders. We'll have a special project and research. Perhaps, someday, I can settle down and lead the botanical garden in Rio or somewhere else in South America. The botanical garden in Rio is very old and very beautiful. It has been open since the early 19th century."

"I had no idea. It all sounds fascinating."

"You should visit someday. We have palm trees that were planted in 1808 when the garden opened. Beautiful. And, what are your educational plans?"

Mari paused before she answered, "I'm not sure right now. I'm still exploring. I love garden design. I wouldn't mind landing somewhere in the US or perhaps in the UK where my grandparents live." She paused, "Have you ever been to the UK?"

He smiled and shook his head, "No, I've never had the pleasure. Perhaps someday, when I tire of the warmth of the Southern Americas."

It sounded a little dramatic, but Mari wasn't sure.

"Did I hear someone say 'warm?'" a sunny voice that matched the long-haired brunette's aura asked as she approached them.

"Hello, Becky," Anastacios greeted.

"Rebecca," she corrected. "Thanks."

She held her hand to Mari and introduced herself, "Rebecca Collins, from warm and sunny Florida. And you?"

Mari couldn't help it; the woman's demeanor was addictive. She laughed and introduced herself. Anastasios excused himself. For a minute, Mari vaguely felt she was on a speed date circuit. But Rebecca was very nice and told her about Koreshan Park and the cult that used to reside there.

"It sounds similar to Ephrata Cloisters," Mari remarked.

"Where's that?"

"In Southern Pennsylvania. It's only a couple of hours from here."

"Hmm, I might need to take a road trip. I do some of the historical interpretation at Koreshan and manage the gardens. It would be great to add to my repertoire." She laughed again.

"And, why Meadowood?" Mari was curious. "Did you know anyone in the program?"

Rebecca shook her head, "Nope. I love my job but needed to stretch my wings a little. Our parks are always on shaky funding. I'm looking to keep my options open in the future. Meadowood's programs are all impressive. I'm a teensy bit jealous of you being able to work on your Master's degree at a botanical garden. Mine was mostly bookwork, with off-site field trips. We didn't live in a gorgeous botanical garden and learn about garden administration and policy."

"It is wonderful. Most of the time, I am deliriously happy. Some days, though, I'm not sure I want to be an indentured servant to Meadowood." She paused and smiled, "But I love it here, so those thoughts pass by quickly."

"That's good to know. This is a pretty fabulous place. I met Dr. Knight at a conference once. He waxed on about Meadowood, as you can imagine."

"I can."

"Nice man. I'm sorry that he's having trouble. I

didn't know Dr. Wellington, and I don't know much about what's happening. A little untoward excitement for this experience."

Mari nodded. A tall man with very round glasses was walking toward them. Rebecca called out to him, "Armand, come and meet Mari."

This was the Belgian guy Sunny spoke of. She didn't see Sunny's attraction to him until he pulled off his glasses. He was drop-dead gorgeous with soulful, chocolate-brown eyes and dark, curly hair. She thought he looked like a combination between Rock Hudson and Harrison Ford. He introduced himself, and she squeaked out a response when she held out her hand. According to Sunny, his passion was building huge automata, but he had the prestigious job of director of horticulture at the Pairi Daiza in Belgium. She was awed and felt tongue-tied.

Dr. Fuller saved her by clanging her glass and announcing, "I hope everyone has had a wonderful time meeting your botanical colleagues at Meadowood. You will likely see one another about the gardens, and now you'll be able to recognize one another. Fellows, if you had a chance to speak with a graduate student with the same interests as yourself for your project, you might choose to collaborate, giving credit where credit is due. Unfortunately, this is all the time we have for our "Meet and Greet." Also, welcome back, Dr. Knight!"

Armand turned away, but Mari hastily said, "A pleasure to meet you, sir. I would like to hear more about Pairi Daiza sometime."

He looked at her again as if seeing her for the first time. "Will do. I look forward to it. Have a pleasant evening."

Mari looked around for Heather. She spied her through the doorway in the vestibule of the mansion.

Mari caught up with her, "Want to take a walk?"

"Sure, down by the cove?"

"That would be great, and then back to the dorm and get those journals written and turned in."

"Work, work, work…" Heather complained good-naturedly. "What did you think of the Meet and Greet?"

"Interesting. Dr. Knight was sure a surprise. But he disappeared quickly at the end."

"He probably wanted to get home!"

"I looked around when he came in the room," Mari added, sotto voce, "and Felicity Kent froze in her spot. I was surprised to see Joe looking upset. Ren looked moody."

Heather commented, "That's odd for Joe, but Ren always looks moody."

"Not always," Mari defended. She looked at Heather, "Well, you're right; most of the time, he seems moody."

"Well, I thought it was odd. Felicity rushed to Dr. Knight when he came in. Her reaction seemed unnatural and disingenuous. It was weird."

"Can you go and talk with Dr. Knight? You do have a personal connection."

"Yeah, maybe after class tomorrow. Assuming we have class."

"It might be a novel thing," Heather teased.

"Yeah, but I don't mind working in the gardens." She paused and looked out at the water. It was a muted Antwerpen blue with navy rivulets of small waves in the breeze. It smelled wonderful and Mari took in deep breaths of the semi-salty air.

"The wind is coming from the south," she remarked as she looked at the water.

"How can you tell?" Heather asked.

"By the tang of salt. Smell. Take in a deep breath."

Heather did as she was told. "You're right. You can catch a hint of an ocean breeze."

"It's stronger the further south you go on the Chesapeake, of course. Where we live in North Bay, the salty air is every so often, but it's a good indicator of whether we will have a bad storm."

"Why?"

"The worst storms come from the south. Like hurricanes and Nor'easters," Mari explained. "Just wait until August. We'll have some brilliant fireworks with lightning."

Heather shivered. "I'm not a fan."

"We should see if we can watch a storm inside the Conservatory later this summer. That would be amazing."

"Only if you bring flashlights and candles."

"Chicken!" Mari teased.

Heather put her hands under her arms, flapping and clucking like a chicken. "Yup, you've got that right."

Mari became serious then and commented, "We need to talk with Joe and find out what's going on and why he's so unhappy with Dr. Knight. And, find out more about Felicity Kent."

"Well, let's head back and get our work done. We can think as we write."

"Spoilsport."

CHAPTER TEN

Mari returned to her room to write her journal entries without much enthusiasm. Her mind kept returning to Joe and Ren's expressions and Dr. Fuller's and Felicity's reactions to Dr. Knight entering the Meet and Greet. She couldn't imagine one of her classmates being a killer. She wondered what connection Felicity Kent had to Dr. Wellington and Dr. Knight. Her reaction had been very odd when he entered the room. And what about Dr. Fuller?

Mari wanted to speak with Felicity again and remembered she had said she would talk with Mari about garden design in the future. Perhaps she would meet Mari for tea? Dr. Fuller promised to send contact information between the Fellows and the Graduate students. When Mari checked her email, there it was. She wrote an email telling Felicity what a pleasure it was to meet her and asked if she would like to get together for tea. Fingers crossed, she pressed 'send.'

Feeling better, she completed her journal entries more enthusiastically than she had begun. After she had completed her tasks, Mari searched for Nepeta and something to eat.

Joe was sitting cross-legged on the couch, eating potato chips and staring at his laptop. He didn't notice the large orange tabby sitting outside and glaring at him. Mari rushed to the door to let Nepeta inside. Should she scold Joe? She decided not to but instead greeted him. He waved a hand with a potato chip in it at her. He was obviously trying to concentrate.

She didn't know what she wanted to eat and rooted around her cupboard and stared into the refrigerator. She didn't feel like cooking. Peanut butter toast sounded all right, however. She popped some bread in the toaster. Nepeta wove around her ankles.

"I'll feed you in my room," she whispered to him as she picked up and him.

He purred in response. The toast popped, and she put him down to spread the peanut butter.

"See you later, Joe," she called as she returned up the stairs.

He grunted.

Mari sat on the window seat to eat her toast, Nepeta putting up a paw to bat at it.

"Stop it!" she scolded. "Let me eat it while it's hot. I'll feed you."

"Miaow," he responded and went to wait by his bowl, staring at it as if it were a black hole. Mari rolled her eyes.

"Okay, okay," she told Nepeta, exasperated. "I'll feed you."

She opened the can of cat food and returned to the window seat. There, she pondered Dr. Wellington's death and wondered who murdered him. She didn't want to think she was living with a murderer under her roof.

Joe and Ren acted odd, but murder? And she still didn't have a clue as to why Joe went from the happy-go-lucky, jock-like fellow to the sullen and angry man. He was very private. When she thought of it, she really didn't know anything about him. She wondered if he opened up more to the guys. Maybe she could ask Franklin, Peter, or even Ren. Ren. What was with him? He was always so moody, but she liked his sense of humor.

Thinking about the murder, she wanted to explore the Felicity Kent angle since she appeared to know both Dr. Knight and Dr. Wellington. She hoped Felicity would get back to her soon. And tomorrow, she hoped she could talk to Dr. Knight. Maybe he would give her some insight on Felicity.

In the meantime, she checked out Felicity on the internet. She was well-known in the UK garden world and had won accolades as one of the top fifty in garden design. She won decorations at the noted Chelsea Garden Show and worked in public spaces, private gardens, and large estates. Mari checked out photos of her designs and liked her use of grasses and natives in her landscapes. Her work was stunning. No wonder she was a Fellow at Meadowood. Didn't she mention something about stretching her wings? No, that was Rebecca Collins. She didn't seem to have any UK connections. She closed her eyes, trying to figure things out.

Nepeta jumped up, breaking her train of thought. He smelled strongly of fishy cat food but ignored her upturned nose and turned in circles to settle onto her lap, purring. She petted him absently, as her head began to ache with the effort of figuring out the murder.

Nepeta protested when she moved him when she decided to take something for her headache. She texted Heather several sites that showcased Felicity's designs.

Heather returned her text with an emoji of a smiley face with hearts for eyes. Heather asked her if she had completed the most recent assignment from Dr. Knight on the cultivars created at Meadowood. She had forgotten about this assignment and texted, "Yikes! I forgot!"

Mari returned to her laptop, writing a well-formed essay on the Meadowood Cultivars would take awhile. A few hours later, she was satisfied with her efforts and sent it to Dr. Knight.

She yawned. It was late when she closed her laptop. It was much later than when she usually went to bed. She crawled into bed with a happy Nepeta and listened to the sounds in the house and outside. Someone was rummaging in the kitchen for a late-night snack. All else seemed quiet. There were a few creaks with the old stables settling.

Outside, she heard the spooky screech owl again. She shivered. She was spooked and wasn't sure why. Nepeta protested, but Mari got up and checked to see that her door was locked. She crawled back into bed, sleep alluding her. Nepeta crawled up by her shoulder. She turned to bury her face in his fur, hoping his presence and purr would lull her to sleep.

Her sleep was restless that night, filled with vivid dreams she could not remember. She woke feeling cranky and went downstairs early, hoping an extra cup of coffee would help her. Ren was in the kitchen. She nodded but didn't greet him.

"What's wrong with you?" Ren asked her when she burned her toast and almost cried.

She looked at him with hollow eyes, "I didn't sleep very well last night."

"What's bothering you?"

"The murder, I think. I know Dr. Knight is innocent.

I keep trying to think of who would want to kill Dr. Wellington or frame Dr. Knight. It doesn't make sense."

"But, Mari, you don't really know either man," Ren said gently. "Maybe they're bastards."

"Dr. Knight? I don't think so... Wellington? I don't know him. Someone from Meadowood has a beef with him. And the police can't figure it out, so that means we have a murderer on the loose."

"We don't know the whole story, Mari. Maybe it was an accident."

"Could it be that simple? That someone was fighting with Dr. Wellington? But, then, who's covering up? That someone needs to tell the police."

When her coffee finished brewing, she took it to an overstuffed armchair, sat down, and sipped. Ren brought her a plate containing sauteed mushrooms and toast. She looked at him gratefully. "Thanks," she told him.

He sat on the sofa next to her chair. "You know," he advised, "leave the wondering to the police. Hopefully, they'll figure out the truth. Maybe there's another reason it happened. We don't have everyone's perspectives."

Her shoulders slumped. "You're right, Ren."

She drained her coffee and turned to him, "My turn to wash up. And I need another cup of coffee, too. You?"

He shook his head. "No. I've been up for a while. I've already had my quota."

Ren disappeared upstairs while she washed up their dishes and brewed a second cup of coffee. She sat and sipped the second cup, thinking about what Ren said. Her imagination wandered, wondering what other perspectives might be plausible.

Dr. Wellington was stabbed. That wasn't an accident. And who stabbed him, and why? She didn't have enough information. And, apparently, the police didn't either. They didn't have evidence to charge Dr. Knight, which was good.

So, what was she missing? Motive, most definitely. She didn't know Dr. Wellington. She heard rumors about his behavior. She observed he was pompous, but she really didn't have a clue why someone would kill him.

She didn't hear Heather until she tapped her on the shoulder and said, "Penny." Mari jumped, nearly spilling her coffee.

"Sorry," Heather apologized.

"No worries. I was lost in thought."

"Apparently. You didn't hear me say your name. I thought you had fallen asleep holding your coffee."

"I think I could have. I didn't sleep well." Mari looked around to see if anyone else was in the common area. Thankfully, it was empty. She turned to Heather, "I've decided I'm very bad at solving mysteries."

"What do you mean?"

"I was talking with Ren. He was saying we didn't have everyone's perspectives on the murder. And, with Dr. Wellington dead, we won't."

"Wait a minute, you discussed this with Ren?"

"Yes and no. He was asking me questions when I was still half asleep. He's right, though. We don't have everyone's perspectives. He was thinking it could have been an accident."

"And, the stabbing?" Heather asked drily.

Mari put her coffee cup down on the table next to her. She buried her head in her hands and moaned, "I am so confused."

"You're right. We don't have all the information. That's why we're asking questions. But, think about it, Mari, how could the death be an accident with a letter opener involved?" Heather questioned.

"It seems like it stemmed more from some argument. And, with the stealing of Dr. Knight's letter opener, wouldn't that be pre-meditated?" Mari's eyes grew wide at the realization.

They heard footsteps. Heather craned her neck but didn't see anyone for a few seconds.

"You're right," she whispered to Mari.

Mari shivered, "So there *is* a murderer at Meadowood."

Heather changed the subject when she saw Peter and Franklin coming down the stairs. She asked Mari brightly, "Do you want some breakfast, Mari?"

"Thanks, no. Ren sauteed some mushrooms and shared them."

"Shrooms. They're the best, man," Peter drawled.

"They are one of my favorites," Mari agreed.

"And they're intelligent plants, except they're not plants," Peter said. "Maybe they're aliens."

He made spooky noises. "I think I might cook some up and eat them in an omelet."

"Cannibal," Heather teased.

Everyone laughed.

"You know," Peter continued, "some scientists think shrooms are more human than plants. There's an ethnobotanist who thinks shrooms are responsible for human intelligence. He thought the spores landed in our brains and are responsible for our intelligence and self-awareness."

"Like the way the one cordyceps fungi takes over ant bodies. The zombie-fungus they call it," Franklin added.

"That's really creepy," Mari said, shivering.

"What's creepy?" Nichelle asked as she entered the common area.

Franklin told her about the zombie-ant fungus.

"Ugh. This is not something I want to discuss before

coffee. I am so tired. I forgot about that essay for Dr. Knight on the Meadowood cultivars until late last night."

"You weren't the only one," Mari sympathized. "I don't usually leave stuff until the last minute like that."

"But you have an excuse," Nichelle insisted, "finding the body and stuff. The stress alone."

"Thanks, I think," Mari retorted.

They bantered back and forth all the way to the Potting Shed. Dr. Fuller was ready with assignments. Mari was assigned to weed at the base of the Clock Tower. Mari blanched when she read the assignment, and Dr. Fuller asked to see her before going to her post.

"I know it will be difficult, Mari," Dr. Fuller began, "but you must face your fears and what you saw. It's like that old saying: if you fall off the horse, you need to get up and get right back on. If it's too much, stop. Just let me know."

Mari gulped and nodded. She wasn't sure what to say to Dr. Fuller. So, she gathered some tools and left the Potting Shed dejectedly. She walked slowly to the Clock Tower.

She walked down the Flower Garden Walk. Sunny and Peter called out to her, "Are you okay?" Mari shrugged. She heard Sunny say something like, "It's too soon. That wasn't very nice of Dr. Fuller."

She continued. Sweat broke out on her forehead. She brushed it away. Mari looked up at the tall, gray tower. The mica in the granite sparkled in the morning sunlight. The chime in the Clock Tower tolled the hour, and her steps slowed to the beat of the bell.

I can do this, she chided herself. *I can do this. I can do this.* She repeated the mantra repeatedly, feeling like "The Little Engine that Could," saying, "I think I can, I think I can." *There's nothing to be afraid of.* Mari gave herself a pep talk. *You've been here hundreds of times with your family.*

She arrived at the base of the Clock Tower. The police tape had been taken away. She looked up, and the bright morning sun came from the back of the tower, nearly blinding her. She imagined Dr Wellington's body on the ground.

Mari took a step back. It was her imagination. She took a deep breath and looked again. There wasn't a body at the bottom of the tower. A soft wind blew around her. The fragrance of the bay and the Flower Garden Walk drifted to her on a soft breeze.

She put down her weed bucket. This area should be fairly clear of weeds due to the police activity. She stepped over the annual blooms in the front with the tall single marigolds, blue salvia, and garnet red begonias. She knelt and smoothed some of the mulch, looking for weeds in the annuals.

Mari spent her time working around the clock tower slowly, saving the area where she found the body last. She hoped it would be time to clean up and go to class before she reached that spot. Alas, the last group of students who weeded did a fine job, so she had little work to do.

She reached the area where the body had lain. New mulch had been scattered. She hesitantly brushed at it, and something caught her eye. It wasn't a piece of mulch, but it was small, rectangular, and brown. She picked it up by the edges and studied it. What was it? Stylized leaves and blossoms were carved into it. It was a flash drive, a fancy one that looked almost like it was carved with a William Morris design. What was it doing here? Had it belonged to Dr. Wellington? She looked at it in wonder at first and then quickly put it in her pocket.

CHAPTER ELEVEN

The Clock Tower chimed, and Mari glanced at the huge clock above her. It was time to go to class. She gathered her things and told herself she would think about the flash drive later. She wondered if she should contact the police.

She was running late, so she hurried to return her tools and jog to the classroom. She was happy to see Dr. Knight in his spot with his cane nearby. When she hurried into the classroom, he bathed her in a benevolent smile. She slid into a seat by Heather.

"I need to talk with you later," she whispered to Heather. "I found something. By the Clock Tower."

Heather's eyebrows raised. She was going to ask a question, but Dr. Knight cleared his throat to begin class. She hurried to pull out her notebook and pen.

Dr. Knight began, "First, I must apologize for the disruption as you began your educational program here at Meadowood. The demise of my long-time colleague, Dr. Alexander Wellington, has been fraught with troubles as the police work to find his killer. I was cordial to Dr. Wellington to prevent any additional rumors, but he was not my friend. We had a falling out many years ago, but that has long since been resolved. I did not kill him. Now, back to plant propagation. Thank you to those who turned in their essays on the Meadowood cultivars. I will begin to go into greater detail about these plants. We'll take a field trip around the gardens, and I can impart additional information about each cultivar. So, gather your things, please. We will begin our journey on the north side of Meadowood by the mediation garden."

The class gathered their things and followed Dr. Knight down the stairs and through the gardens. Visitors were starting to arrive and were also streaming out the doors to the garden areas. Dr. Knight led them by the mansion, through the sensory and bonsai gardens, where he smiled reverently at the older trees and onward to the Meditation Garden.

On the way, Heather stuck close to Mari.

"You found what at the Clock Tower?"

"A flash drive," she told Heather quietly.

"What are you going to do with it?"

Mari shrugged before answering, "I don't know. I don't know if I should look at it or turn it in to the police or both. I mean you always hear about those things infecting computers. Anyways, if it has to do with the murder, I shouldn't be looking at it at all!"

She looked around a little nervously and wondered if anyone had heard her. Ren was looking at his phone. Peter was whistling and looking around. Sunny and Nichelle were chatting. Joe and Franklin were talking.

Near the rear of the garden, in the partial shade of the woods, Dr. Knight stopped by a tall evergreen bush with dark, leathery leaves. He almost grinned before stating, "A drumroll, please."

The group looked a little confused.

"May I present to you the Lady Anna Camellia. It was named for Lady Anna Elizabeth Blackthorn. Camellia Japonica. And, although it looks like a dark evergreen bush at this time of year, in the winter, it will blossom with sweetly scented blossoms of ivory that age to a lovely pink hue. It's a winter pick-me-up, and this particular cultivar blooms profusely. What can you tell me about camellias?" he asked the group.

Ren raised his hand. "Camellia Japonica is related to Camellia Sinensis, the tea plant. Both are tender, and they need to grow in milder conditions."

"Very good, Ren."

"Their bloom time is in the winter," Nichelle added tentatively. "I think from December, for some varieties, until April. Their blossoms are classic. I tend to think of them as a Southern flower."

"Excellent, Nichelle."

"This cultivar, as I mentioned earlier, was in danger of extinction. Meadowood tweaked the endangered plant and created a new cultivar besides."

"This next plant, Hydrangea Paniculata, 'Time and Again' is also a cultivar of Meadowood. As you can see, it's a lovely lace-cap hydrangea with large conical heads. It's a very popular plant with our pollinators. It's called 'Time and Again,' because the petals change from pale green to white to pink and finally red in the autumn. The dried heads keep their dark color and are prized for dried arrangements. We have several here and more by the Clock Tower."

He smiled as the clock chimed the hour.

"Unfortunately, we are out of time for this morning, but I want to meet you in the Conservatory this afternoon to continue this discussion. After this afternoon's lecture, please enlighten me with a short essay on the importance of cultivars and which cultivar or cultivars you are most interested in."

Dr. Knight strode off down the Woodland Walk, his cane clacking lightly on the pathway, leaving the students to stare after him.

"I wonder where he's going?" Peter asked and joked, "Maybe he has a stash in the woods."

"Oh, Peter," Sunny sighed, "Get a grip."

Mari thought she knew where he was going. She thought Dr. Knight and Boothby likely knew each other well.

Heather tugged Mari's elbow, "Show me where you found the flash drive," she insisted.

Mari tried to look casual and walk towards the Clock Tower.

"This is tough for me," she told Heather. "I wasn't sure I could work here this morning. I – I," she stopped.

"I'm sorry," Heather relented. "If it's too tough, we can go another way."

"N-no. I need to be able to face this place," Mari stuttered, "and to stop seeing Dr. Wellington's body."

"Ouch."

They walked on a semi-shaded path. The blossoms of the Kousa dogwood around the Clock Tower had blown prettily across the paths and lawn areas. They stopped at the base of the tower and looked up. The rest of the students seemed to follow them, so Mari couldn't say anything to Heather but nodded at the garden in front of them. Heather seemed to understand. Mari touched her pocket to make sure the flash drive was still there. Mari took a breath and made herself move from the spot.

Back at the dorm, she checked her email. Felicity

had responded and asked if she could come to tea at her cottage that afternoon. Mari quickly replied she would come at four. She would take one of her precious bottles of Grandad's cider as a gift. That should sweeten the pot.

She ran into Heather in the kitchen trying to recreate the spicy chickpea mixture they had the previous day at the 'Meet and Greet.' She kept consulting her phone and staring into her cupboard.

"Do you have any sumac?" Heather whined.

"Actually, I do. I use it when I make chickpea salad sometimes. Let me get it for you."

Mari rooted in her cupboard and handed the jar to Heather.

Heather added some sumac to the dish and stirred. She tasted it again.

"Close. Not quite the same as yesterday's mixture, but it's pretty good."

"If you want to share, I can toast these tortillas. They puff up like pita bread, and we can fill them with your creation."

"Sounds like a plan," Heather agreed.

She filled Heather in on visiting Felicity for tea.

"Are you sure you want to go alone since we're suspecting she is involved with Dr. Wellington's death?"

"I think I'll be all right. I have my phone, and I'll sit near the door, okay?"

"As long as you don't think she'll poison you," Heather said darkly.

"Now, who is being dramatic!"

They said all this in whispers. Joe was at the other end of the kitchen island.

"Why all the secrets?" he asked, "Solving the mysteries of the world?"

"Only murders," Heather quipped.

Mari blanched and elbowed Heather in the ribs. Joe shook his head.

"Right," he said sarcastically, but he threw the remains of his lunch away and stalked off.

"What's eating him?" Nichelle asked as Joe blew past her on the steps.

"I don't know. And they say women are moody," Heather said.

"Huh, clearly they haven't been in this dorm," Nichelle added.

The girls laughed.

"Hey, Sunny and I are headed to town later. Want to come? We could have a girls' night."

"I'm sorry, I can't. I want to talk to Felicity Kent about garden design. I think that will be my main focus," Mari informed her.

"She's a good one to tap into," Nichelle agreed. "Heather? Will you tag along?"

Heather gave Mari a long look. Mari smiled and nodded.

"Okay. I will."

Dr. Knight's lecture that afternoon focused on several tropical cultivars attributed to the horticulturalists at Meadowood. Mari found the lecture interesting, but she was anxious to meet Felicity and wondered what she would say to her.

As soon as the lecture was over, she raced back to the dorm to change and get a bottle of cider. She tied a ribbon around the neck of the bottle. She texted Heather goodbye and asked her to wish her luck.

Outside, she walked around the side of the dormitory and to a path that paralleled the parking lot. It led Mari past the wooded area to a row of small houses. They were older duplex homes built at the turn of the century for the Meadowood employees of days gone by. Felicity had messaged her that she was in the next to the last house. The duplexes were back from the road that led to Oak Harbor with private access. Oyster shells were used for hardscaping the path and driveway, like many of the paths at Meadowood. Mari knew it was an economical as well as environmental piece of landscaping.

Mari walked up to the duplex, where pots of bright geraniums and other annuals graced the porch. The windows were open, and classical music was playing softly somewhere inside. She knocked. After a few moments, Mari heard footsteps, and Felicity opened the door.

"Come in! Come in!" she welcomed and beckoned Mari inside the house. "It's so lovely to have someone understand having a spot of tea in the afternoon."

Mari could smell baking, so she followed Felicity to the kitchen. There, Felicity opened the oven to check on something inside. She pulled the tray from the oven, revealing perfectly baked scones. Mari's mouth watered. They smelled like her grandmother's scones.

"Please, sit down," Felicity gestured to the kitchen table, which had been set with two plates, cups, cream, and sugar. A teapot, covered in a hand-knitted cozy, sat in the center of the table. Butter and jam were also on the table. Mari sat.

"I'm sorry I cannot get clotted cream here in the States. We'll have to make do with butter and jam."

"This smells just like my grandparents' kitchen. Thank you for making tea. And I brought you something from home."

"What's that?" Felicity asked as she brought a dish filled with warm scones to the table. They were covered in a tea towel to hold in the heat.

Mari held out the bottle of cider.

"Oh, my! Where did you find that? What a prize!"

Mari laughed at Felicity's delight. "It's from my grandfather's cidery."

"Oh! How lucky you are. It's one of my favorite ciders, and you can't get it here."

"Don't I know it," Mari added.

"What a treat. I'll save this for something special."

Felicity poured the tea, and they each added their cream and sugar. She gestured to Mari to take a scone, and Mari did so. They were light and fluffy; steam escaped when she pulled the scone apart. She slathered it with butter, which melted quickly into the crumb, and topped it with jam.

"These are heavenly," Mari told Felicity at the first bite. "I didn't think anyone could come close to my grandmother's scones, but yours are perfect."

Felicity blushed a little, "I learned from my grandmother. It's not hard."

They ate their scones in companionable silence for a few minutes when Felicity asked, "You mentioned your interest in garden design?"

"Yes, I wondered how you got started?"

"Well, I came upon it by chance. I'm a botanist and spent many years in academia as a professor. My funding was cut, and I was out of a job. Fortunately, I took a bit of the severance and started a business. Loving and knowing plants is the best foundation. Studying the great gardens is helpful, too."

"Wait a minute, you lost your job as a professor due to funding cuts?"

Felicity nodded. "Funds were transferred from my department to another for their innovative research."

"That's terrible!"

"Yes, it was. Two of us lost our jobs, thanks to Alex.

My other colleague never recovered and drowned himself in drink. It killed him."

Mari ventured to ask, "Alex, as in Dr. Alexander Wellington?"

"The same."

"My grandad refers to him as a 'bad one.'"

"Really? What does he do in the botany world?"

Mari realized she had let too much slip and backpedaled, "Nothing really; well, he's involved with apples and the harvest for the cider. I think he met Dr. Wellington at some events."

"Hmm." Felicity sipped at her tea.

Mari hoped she believed her.

"Trust me, between you and me, I'm not exactly upset at his demise. Whoever did that to him did me a favor," Felicity said darkly but then changed the subject and directed advice to Mari, "My advice to you is to learn as much as possible at Meadowood, even under that crazy old coot, Artie Knight. He's good, but has a screw loose about King Arthur, if you haven't noticed. Look for internships and opportunities after your degree and see if you can spread your wings internationally. Work on design while you're here. Apply for any awards and prizes you can as a student. They will all stack up on your CV. But, overall, learn about plants, plant diseases, and how they can best survive. That way, your designs will be sustainable."

"That sounds like good advice. After finishing at Meadowood, I hope to spend significant time in the UK with my grandparents. Perhaps I can find some opportunities there."

She wasn't exactly lying. It was an idea she had tossed around.

"Then, look me up," Felicity insisted. "We'll be in

contact here, and I'll be easily reached in the future."

"Thank you for having me to tea. It was wonderful."

"Any time," Felicity said, "We Brits need to stick together. Well, most of us," she added as an aside.

Mari pretended she didn't hear the last remark. Her head was spinning with all she had heard.

CHAPTER TWELVE

Mari returned to the dorm and lay on her bed, thinking about what Felicity said. Nepeta tromped around her, purring, and licked her nose. Eventually, he settled on her chest. She stroked his head. It had been lovely to have a British tea despite the revelations from Felicity. She didn't respect Dr. Knight. And she clearly had a motive to kill Dr. Wellington. She wondered if the police knew.

Mari wanted to talk to Heather. She texted her, asking if she was back at Meadowood.

"We're at the pub. Join us!" Heather texted back.

"No, thanks. I'll talk to you about what I learned when you get back," Mari texted.

Heather sent her a thumbs-up emoji. Mari sensed they were having a good time but didn't want to join them. Her head was still filled with questions. Could Felicity Kent have killed Dr. Wellington? She wasn't an overly large woman, but in anger, Mari thought she could pack a good wallop, especially if he wasn't expecting it. But why the letter opener? Did she take it because she didn't like Dr. Knight? The theory fit together.

Mari was fidgety. She wondered when Heather, Sunny, and Nichelle would get back. But, it was Friday night, and she suspected they were letting off a little steam. Part of her wanted to be with them; she was also restless. She took Nepeta off her chest and put him on the bed.

"I'll be back in a few minutes," she told the cat. "I want to take a walk."

Downstairs, Ren was eating at the kitchen island. He nodded at her when she walked past. Peter, Joe, and Franklin were gaming on the community television. She ignored her growling stomach and walked to the path to the clock tower.

Mari wanted to figure out how Dr. Wellington died. She hadn't been up in the Clock Tower in a couple of years. She and her family liked to climb the inside spiral stairs to see the view from the balcony. She approached the door only to find it padlocked and shook the large padlock on the door in frustration.

She heard Dr. Knight had been at the Clock Tower that night, remembering her conversation with her grandfather, who said Detective Booker let it slip But, had Felicity? Was it a reunion of three British colleagues? Dr. Knight left. He likely couldn't climb the narrow spiral stairs inside the tower. But what about Felicity? Did she lure Dr. Wellington up the stairs? It was plausible. Or did she meet him at the base of the tower? And, what about the flash drive? Did it belong to Dr. Wellington, or maybe Felicity Kent? That was a possibility too.

She hadn't heard from Detective Booker in a couple of days. She wondered if she would and then chided herself. She needed to let him know about finding the flash drive. It was almost seven, and it was too late to call tonight. She doubted he was still at the Police Station. Even though it was the weekend, she could do it in the morning.

The afternoon heat still hung heavily in the air. Mari turned to the Woodland Path to return to the dorm. Walking the forested path calmed her a little, but the questions still swirled in her head. The forest was thick in spots, and the clusters of trees made deep, dark shadows. The pathway was dusky with low-level lighting. There was only enough light to see the path. She had to be careful where she was going.

It was the time of evening when everything was quiet. The birds were quiet except for a loud osprey screeching somewhere near the Bay. Mari heard the crack of a stick. She stopped. Everything was still. She walked on a little farther, her senses now alert. Was someone behind her? Was someone following her?

"Hello?" her voice quavered a little. "Who's out there?"

The sun was setting, and she could see the colors through the trees and across the Bay. But that meant it was getting darker on the Woodland Path. She quickened her pace. She was sure she heard footsteps behind her. She kept glancing over her shoulder, seeing nothing, but her anxiety rose. Her heart pounded in her chest. She started to walk and then jog faster along the path, praying she wouldn't trip.

Suddenly, in the dusk, stood Boothby's cottage. With a sob and a wash of relief, she went up to the gate. She was trembling from head to toe.

"Boothby? Are you there? It's Mari? Boothby?" her voice quavered as she called out.

The old man came to the gate. He looked as if he had been asleep.

"Mari! What a pleasant surprise! Come in," he said, opening the gate. I confess I must have fallen asleep in my garden. Unfortunately, it happens a lot more these days." He chuckled at himself.

He didn't seem to notice how distraught she was. Mari was happy to be safely inside his walled garden area. She knew something was out there. She knew it wasn't good. Someone had been following her.

Boothby led her inside his charming cottage. It wasn't overly large but cozy with post and beam construction, an open seating area, and a kitchen layout. Near the fireplace was an old, wingback chair and a small table stacked with a few books, leaving little space for the small, rounded lamp. There were bookshelves near the fireplace and also in the living room. She was itching to see the titles.

Boothby invited her to sit at a well-worn kitchen table. The table had to be an antique, and the mismatched chairs looked handmade. In the kitchen area, herbs hung from the beams. Mari saw a hallway that she assumed led to the bedroom and bathroom.

"Care for a spot of tea? I grow my own, you know. The Camellia Sinensis likes the warmth of my brick walls. And I keep them protected in the winter."

"Thank you. I would love some," Mari told him, starting to relax a little. "You said you grow your own tea?"

"Yup, grow it, dry it, and drink it. Artie likes his imported stuff, and I like my own. We like to argue about it."

He turned on an electric kettle and took out a teapot. When the water was hot, he filled the teapot with hot water to warm it. She was happy he warmed the teapot before adding the tea leaves and more water to make the tea properly. He filled the kettle again and turned it on.

"You know Dr. Knight?"

"Of course! He's been at Meadowood nearly as long as I have."

"I think you would like my grandad. He's a friend of Dr. Knight's, too."

"I believe I would," Boothby said. "So, what brings you to my doorstep this lovely spring evening?"

Mari flushed, "I was taking a walk, and I became a little spooked."

"From this murder business?"

She nodded, "I think I was being followed on the Woodland Walk. I panicked. And then your house appeared."

"I am glad to be of service," Boothby told her.

The kettle whistled. He dumped the water out of the teapot, added a strainer with dried leaves from a jar, and poured the boiling water over this.

"We need to let it steep a few minutes," he said and covered the teapot with a cozy.

He pulled down two mugs and a small plate. From a cupboard, he pulled down a tin.

"My weakness," he told Mari, and she smiled as he put shortbread cookies on a plate.

She jumped up to help him bring things to the table.

"Will you pour?" he asked.

She did. Mari loved the tea's fresh, grassy, nutty, almost floral aroma. Boothby handed her the plate of shortbread. She took one and nibbled at it. Her stomach growled, betraying her hunger. Boothby heard.

"Are you hungry? Do you want something other than a cookie or two?"

Mari was embarrassed, "No," she insisted. "I'll be fine."

"Will you?"

She sipped the hot tea, drawing the mug back quickly as it burned her lips.

"It's this murder. I can't figure it out, and it's driving me crazy."

"Is it your problem to figure out? Isn't that the job of the police?"

Mari flushed, "I know. I was originally interested because they took Dr. Knight. As I said, he's a friend of my grandad's, you see. There's no way Dr. Knight could have killed Dr. Wellington, even if he was with him that night."

"You're right there. Artie is a peaceful man. Conflict is something he abhors."

"I think that's why I like him so much. He exudes calmness and peace."

"He would love to hear that. You'll have to tell him sometime."

"I know, but I'm his student. And that isn't very easy because he knows Grandad. I'm trying to keep that secret because I don't want anyone thinking I'm getting any favors."

"I can see where that would be difficult."

"A couple of the students seem 'off' in a way, but I can't see them going after Dr. Wellington. Felicity Kent is a Fellow from the UK. She knows Dr. Knight and Dr. Wellington. She has a motive." Mari said, spilling out her suspicions.

"Does she now?" Boothby stroked his chin.

"So, Felicity, Dr. Wellington, and Dr. Knight know one another. That's another wrinkle. I don't know," she ended with exasperation.

Mari blew on her tea and took a tentative sip. She loved the light, nutty flavor.

"This is delicious."

"Thank you."

"Did you know Dr. Wellington?"

"I knew of him but never met the bastard."

Her eyes flew to his.

"You heard me. I know about his shenanigans years ago with Artie. I suspect he wasn't the only one. It seems to me that a man like Wellington thrived on using people. Someone just got fed up with it."

"You're probably right."

She squirmed a little in her seat and felt a pinch in her pocket. The flash drive. She winced.

"What's wrong?"

"They sent me out to weed at the Clock Tower this morning with the theory that it was like falling off a horse and needing to get back on."

"What in the blazes?" Boothby interrupted, incensed. "You found a body. That's upsetting enough! Who was it? Fuller?"

She nodded.

"Of course, it had to be Fuller. That sounds just like her."

"I think she meant well," Mari said gently.

"Perhaps, but not very tactful."

Mari couldn't help it and laughed. "I don't think tact is a strong suit for her."

"You're right there. She's a good woman, in any case. And she knows her stuff about trees. Without her, Meadowood's trees would be at a loss. She's created a world-renowned tree collection here. Watch her with the trees. She's a different woman."

"Hmm. That would be nice to see. She mostly barks at the students."

Boothby laughed, "I can see that. And she loves her coffee the way I love tea."

"She's never without it." Mari ate another cookie.

A small clock on the mantle chimed, and she realized it was getting late.

"Thank you. Thank you for the tea, cookies, and conversation and for calming me down. But I need to be getting back to the dorm."

"I hope you're not thinking of walking back alone after you told me you thought someone was following you," Boothby chided.

"I guess I was because I have already put you in so much trouble."

"No trouble at all, m'dear. I appreciate your company. I'll walk you back. Let me get a torch. It's getting dark."

It wasn't far to the dorm, and for as ancient as Boothby was, he was spry. They didn't see or hear anything odd as they walked the short distance from his cottage to the dorm.

"My, how this has changed," he commented when they reached the door. "I remember when it used to be stables."

"Would you like to come in?" Mari offered.

"Thank you, not this evening," Boothby answered.

"All right then. Thank you again, Boothby." Mari gave him a quick kiss on the cheek.

"Any time, m'dear." He smiled, tipped his hat, and returned to his cottage.

Mari went inside. No one was in the common area. She climbed the stairs to her room and opened her door to an anxious cat. He wound around her legs, meowing.

"It's okay, Nepeta. I'm okay. It was scary, though. Boothby took care of me."

Nepeta purred.

CHAPTER THIRTEEN

Mari woke, remembering it was the weekend, and stretched luxuriously. She didn't have to get up. She didn't have classes or work in the garden. And, she was at Meadowood. It was still early, and visitors weren't on the grounds. Nepeta stretched too, his long body pressed against her and his paw just reaching her cheek.

"Lazy cat," she teased him.

He purred.

"I think I am going to take a walk, Nepeta. That is before the visitors are here."

Mari made a large mug of coffee and pulled a breakfast bar from her cupboard, realizing she didn't have dinner last night. She stepped out into the sunshine, trying to decide where to go first. One of her dreams was to be at Meadowood without the crowds.

She wandered through the labyrinth, sipping her coffee as she followed the path, and then walked to the water. She looked back at the Blackthorn mansion. It was quite a sight with the sun behind it. It almost sparkled in the early morning sunshine, and the windows reflected the gardens, sky, and cove.

She continued to walk to the Meadow Garden, which was already buzzing with pollinators and birds. Reading the informational signs about beneficial insects, she thought of Heather. She pulled out her phone and texted her. No response. It wasn't that early—it was eight a.m. She called.

Heather's voice answered in a croak.

Mari winced, "Sorry, I didn't think I would wake you."

"S'okay," Heather's voice was a little slurry. "Stayed out way too late. Headache."

"I'm in the Meadow Garden and walking to the Meditation Garden. Want to meet me?"

"Yes. No. I guess."

Mari laughed.

"Don't laugh too loud, okay?"

"See you in a few minutes."

Mari left the Meadow Garden and walked to the Children's Garden. It had taken on various forms over the years. She liked the most recent renovation, where there was a playground structure in the shape of an old sailing ship. Small automatic fountains played around the ship. Mari took off her flip-flops and wandered through the small, playful fountains. It was built to represent Lord Blackthorn's contribution to the sailing industry, and the small fountains represented the water of the Chesapeake Bay. Educational signage, comfortable benches for parents, and stroller parking were available. She remembered that when she was small there had been a honeybee theme. She remembered honey-bee hop-scotch through a hive and bee dances marked on stepping stones leading from large flower sculptures to the hive playground structure. What fun she had with her brother and sister there.

When she walked through, one of Meadowood's workers was watering the Sensory Garden. She appreciated the scents of the herbaceous plants. She let her fingers trail the textures and wispy foliage of the fountain grasses at the outer edge of the garden as she made her way to the Meditation Garden.

Mari sat on a bench in the Meditation Garden, closed her eyes, and sipped her coffee. She listened to the tinkling sound of the fountain. The colors and arrangement of the Meditation garden plants created areas where people could sit and contemplate. There was a central fountain, and Japanese Boxwood defined areas where there was seating. Mari knew her sister would drive to Meadowood to find a spot to read for the day. She knew the Meditation Garden was one of her favorite spots, the bench near the weeping willow. Lacy Japanese Maples and swaying Hakone grass accented the contemplative areas. Like many other spots at Meadowood, crushed oyster shells covered the ground, showcasing the plantings. Mari knew the oyster shells were from the local Chesapeake Bay oyster industry, and it was one of Meadowood's tributes to the Eastern Shore and was environmentally sound. She heard footsteps approach, crunching on the shells, and her eyes flew open.

Heather was walking toward her, coffee in hand and wearing large sunglasses.

"Hey," Mari greeted. "How are you doing?"

"I'm okay," Heather told her. "Not as lively as I would like to be."

"I was thinking of going to town to the Farmers' Market. Want to come?"

"I guess so, as long as we can stop for more coffee."

"There's coffee, fresh vegetables, yummy baked goods, plants, and all kinds of good stuff. Let's stop back at the dorm in a few minutes to get hats and sunblock."

They sat for a few minutes enjoying the peaceful garden when Heather commented, "This is really nice."

"Another time, we'll have to come to read or study here," Mari suggested.

"I can see that," Heather agreed. Mari stood up and held a hand to pull Heather from the bench, ordering, "Come on, girlfriend."

Heather grunted, and they returned to the dorm to grab hats and sunblock before heading to the parking lot to get into Mari's car. It was a lovely drive in the early morning sun to Oak Harbor.

When they arrived, Oak Harbor was bustling, and Mari drove around desperately seeking parking. Finally, someone pulled out of a space a few blocks from the Farmers' Market. It was a side street, more like an alley, but it had parking.

The waterside park was filled with vendor tents. Mari first led Heather to the bakery nearby for more coffee and baked treats. Mari was a sucker for their Raspberry Cinnamon rolls, which were warm and gooey with icing. Her grandmother made incredible cinnamon-twist buns and these rolls were the closest thing to Nan's that she found. Tasting the roll filled with butter, sugar, and raspberry filling flooded her with memories of being with Nan and Grandad. She missed them.

Caffeinated and sugared, they walked to the park and perused the vendors' offerings. Mari picked up local eggs, radishes, mushrooms, and fresh strawberries, while Heather picked up salad greens, spring onions, and hydroponic tomatoes.

After shopping, they sat on a small bench overlooking the water. The tide was low, and Heather was enchanted by the small snails that had crawled up on the bordering grasses. They sat quietly for a few minutes.

"You never told me about the Luna Moth project, Heather."

"Oh, th-a-t," she drawled out the words. "It's a great idea, but not feasible. Luna Moths, once their hatched, only live a week. They don't even have mouths. They're put on earth to mate, lay eggs, and look ethereal and beautiful. I told Dr. Fuller that a Butterfly House would be a better idea. I'm talking her into a Butterfly House and, perhaps, an insectarium exhibit for my graduation project."

"Geez, you're thinking ahead."

"I wouldn't have unless they hadn't approached me about the Luna Moths. I did share an artist who makes lifelike paper Luna Moth models with Dr. Fuller. We could place those in the exhibit."

"That would be pretty."

"Now, catch me up on the news from your end. Did you call the police about the flash drive? Did you talk to Felicity Kent?"

"I forgot to call Detective Booker. I need to do that. But it's the weekend."

"Do it now so that you don't forget again."

"Yes, Mom," she drawled. She pulled out her phone to dial and, as usual, left a message for Detective Booker.

"And, your meeting with Felicity Kent?"

"It went well. She made fresh scones. I was transported to the UK for a few minutes. She has a motive. Dr. Wellington was the cause of her losing funding and her job at her university. She thinks Dr. Knight is a cuckoo."

"Wow."

"But I also didn't tell you someone was following

me last night."

"Last night? What do you mean?"

"I went for a walk to figure some of this out. I went to the Clock Tower and discovered they chained it shut."

"What?" Heather interjected.

Mari nodded and continued, "Then I walked along the Woodland Path. It's so peaceful there."

Heather made a motion for Mari to hurry it up.

"Okay, okay, anyways, I heard a twig snap. I called out, and no one answered."

"It could have been a deer or a squirrel."

"Not one with two feet walking behind me when I moved on," Mari added darkly.

"What did you do?"

"I ran up to Boothby's cottage. He let me in, made me tea, and walked me back to the dorm."

"That's unbelievable. Do you think someone thinks you're getting too close to the answer?"

"I don't know. It was scary, though."

"Hey, look, there's Felicity Kent."

"Where?"

"Buying strawberries from that vendor over there," Heather pointed to a bright green tent.

Mari caught Felicity's eye and waved to her. Felicity walked over to greet Heather and Mari.

"What a glorious day! Look at those beautiful sailboats." She pointed to the bay.

"There must be a regatta," Mari explained, looking at the number of boats on the water. "The Farmers Market is fun, isn't it?"

"Delightful," Felicity agreed.

"Have you tried the bakery?" Heather offered. "We just came from there. It's dangerously delicious."

"Ooh, I'll have to stop by."

"Their scones aren't as nice as yours," Mari complimented.

"Aren't you sweet. Thank you."

"Just being honest. Your scones yesterday reminded me of Nan's. But the bakery's cinnamon buns are close to Nan's twists."

"Good advice."

Felicity's phone rang. "I must take this," she told the girls. She waved goodbye.

As she walked away, the girls overheard her say, "Yes, about the research files…"

Their eyes grew wide.

"I wonder…" Mari murmured.

"You have to get that flash drive to the police."

"I know, but I don't trust Detective Parker. I want to give it to Detective Booker personally."

"I can understand that." Changing the subject, Heather asked, "Where's a good place to go swimming?"

"Betterton Beach is just up the road. It's probably full at this time of day. I can show you where it is, though. People find really old sea glass there from the 19th century. Sometimes, there are food trucks. It's a pretty nice beach. You can grill."

"We should get the gang to go some weekend."

"That would be fun. Maybe it would get Joe out of his bad mood."

"That would be a miracle. I don't know what happened to him. It's like he's a Dr. Jekyll and Mr. Hyde."

They walked around town and stopped by the bookstore to hang out with McTavish. Mr. Howard spotted Mari and came over to her.

"Mari, I have a couple of books that came in that you might like. Let me go to the office to get them." Heather looked at her, puzzled.

"We've been coming here for years. Mr. Howard knows all of our tastes in books in our family and probably for most of the town. He's amazing."

Mr. Howard returned and handed Mari two red leather-bound books. The titles of the books were *Wayside & Woodland Blossoms* and *A Guide to British Wildflowers*. Mari sucked in a breath. They were in pristine condition save for a few penciled notes. The illustrations were lovely botanical watercolors.

"Oh, oh, oh!" Mari cried softly. She looked up at Mr. Howard, and happy tears filled her eyes.

He noticed and cleared his throat. "I remembered you said you went to the UK often. Do your grandparents live there? Did I remember that correctly?"

She nodded, working to control her emotions. Finally, she said, "Thank you. These are gorgeous! Of course, I want them."

"Good. I'm glad you like them." He snapped his fingers. "McTavish," he ordered, "take these to the counter."

Mr. Howard handed McTavish a handled basket. McTavish took it gently in his teeth and trotted up to the counter. The young clerk praised him and gave him a small dog biscuit. He wagged his long, large tail. Heather and Mari laughed.

After poking around the town, Heather suggested picking up something from the sub shop where they had previously eaten. They returned to Mari's car and went to the shopping center.

Mari drove Heather to Betterton Beach, where they picnicked, finding a spot on the crowded sand. Heather was enchanted with the small beach and amazed that the town didn't have more of a tourist presence.

"It's been this way as long as I can remember. I think it's been around, with boarding houses, since Victorian times."

"I want to come back earlier in the day so we can grab a good spot on the beach and maybe a grill," Heather requested.

"Sure. That would be great. Do you want to ask Nichelle and Sunny, and then another time, with the guys as well?"

Heather agreed. "We had a great time last night. I'm sorry you didn't join us, but I understand."

"Thanks. Maybe next time."

Mari drove the small winding roads back toward Meadowood. There was only one short stretch of four-lane highway. At this juncture, an idiot who was tailgaiting her sped around her. She turned onto the narrow road that led to Meadowood. It was curvy, and going South, the road dropped off to the bay. A couple of scenic outlooks were off to the side.

Without warning, a large truck drifted into her lane as it headed north. Mari sounded the horn, swerved, and braked hard.

"That was crazy," Heather said.

Mari was a little spooked. She wanted to return to Meadowood as soon as possible, so she sped up. When she did, she felt the car twist beneath her hands. She and Heather heard a loud pop, and the car veered out of control.

"Oh my God!" Heather screamed.

Mari did all she could to keep the car on the road. It was difficult. The steering wheel seemed to have a life of its own, and she gripped it with iron will. They had been going downhill. The car clunked and bumped loudly. Her tire. She could finally slow to a stop and pull off the road. She sat for a minute, unable to release her hands from the steering wheel.

"What happened?" Heather asked.

"I don't know. Let's look."

When they got out of the car, they found the tread pulled away and hanging loosely from the front driver's side tire. It had blown.

"Your tire's blown out!" Heather cried.

"It looks that way," Mari said grimly. "But I don't know why. My tires are good. Ugh, I hate changing tires."

"You know how?"

She nodded. "My dad made me learn."

"That's a good skill to know."

Mari opened the trunk and pulled out the spare and the tire jack. Heather assisted when asked, and in a few minutes, the spare was on, and the damaged tire was in the trunk.

"Look, I can take you back to Meadowood, but I want to find a place to fix this today."

"Okay, I'll go with you."

Mari used her phone to find a repair shop. She called and explained what happened. Then, she and Heather returned to Oak Harbor.

"The man said he would work us in," Mari explained.

It was a bit of a wait at the tire place. Heather took a walk, and Mari looked at her new books. She was delighted that the previous owner had penciled in the locations where she found the wild flowers. She would need to tuck these books into her suitcase on her next trip to the UK. She knew her Nan would love these books and delight in the same things Mari found charming about them.

Mark, the tire guy, interrupted her thoughts. She looked up when he said her name and he didn't look happy.

"You had quite the blow-out, Miss Mari. Blow-outs

are usually caused by impact damage, big cuts that can lead to air loss or overloading. I thought you might have run over something in the road."

"I don't remember anything," she told him.

He nodded and brought out a piece of tread. "It looks like someone put a big nail between your treads," he indicated a hole. "It wouldn't happen immediately, but it looks like it worked loose and caused a blow-out."

"You mean this was deliberate?"

"I think so. I am sorry."

Mari shook her head. "I don't know why someone would do that."

And then realization hit her: perhaps someone thought she was getting too close to the killer. But she wasn't! She was completely confused. Now, she really wanted to talk to Detective Booker. She texted Heather to return to the tire place.

"Thank you," she told Mark and settled the bill.

"You be careful, Miss Mari."

"Thanks," she said faintly.

She was distracted and went to her car to wait for Heather. Heather came bouncing up and slid into her seat.

"All fixed? I found this great chocolate shop. I thought we could use a treat after that scare."

She pulled out a box and opened it to reveal a variety of light and dark chocolates hand-painted with beautiful designs.

"Oh, Heather, I needed this more than you'll ever know."

"Why? Was the bill terrible?' She reached in and snagged a chocolate after Mari had chosen.

Mari finished her first chocolate and reached for a second. Before she put the second chocolate in her mouth, she told Heather, "My car was sabotaged."

"What?"

Mari nodded, "Mark, the guy at the tire shop, said someone put a large nail or something in between the treads so that the tire would blow out at some point. And it did. We were lucky."

"I'll say. That's another thing to mention to your cute Detective Booker."

"He's not *my* detective."

"Well, maybe he could be," Heather said hopefully.

"Oh... you!" Mari returned and started the car to return to Meadowood.

CHAPTER FOURTEEN

"I think I want to spend the rest of the day reading and relaxing," Mari told Heather. "I've had enough excitement."

"And I want a nap," Heather yawned between words.

It seemed as though everyone had exited the dorm this weekend. The building was quiet—almost too quiet. Mari had gotten used to the eight humans wandering about and living together. After they put their groceries away, Heather told Mari she was heading upstairs to nap and that it might be tomorrow when she saw her.

Mari went up to her room. Nepeta was in his favorite spot on the window seat. She joined him and looked out over the gardens. It was a lovely early summer's day. A light breeze from the water ruffled her curtains. The gardens were crowded and would be open until ten tonight. She thought there was a concert scheduled in the amphitheater. She would need to check the website. She liked her bird's-eye view of the gardens. The visitors' sounds were muffled except for an occasional shriek from a child.

Mari sighed happily and opened the books she had picked up at the bookstore today. She was touched that Mr. Howard had remembered her interests and put them aside. They were lovely volumes. There was a faded, inked name inside the front cover. The first name was Harriet. She couldn't read the last name. The publication date of the books was 1931, and Mari wondered when Harriet purchased them. From the notes penciled in the volumes, it was clear she had taken the wildflower guidebooks on her trips throughout the British Isles. Harriet had made notations of where she located the wildflowers. Mari leafed through the books, looking for Harriet's notations. She had been to several of the same spots Harriet had visited. She thought she would like to take these guidebooks to continue the notations and go on wildflower searches with Nan on her next trip.

Suddenly, her stomach growled so loudly that Nepeta opened his eyes.

"Okay," she told him, "I'll go and make dinner."

The common area was still quiet. She sauteed some vegetables and scrambled eggs, adding some local cheese she had picked up at the Farmers' Market.

Nepeta was very interested when she returned to her room with her bowl. He sniffed at it eagerly.

"You're a mooch," she scolded him but put a bit of egg and cheese on the floor for him to eat.

He ignored her scolding but instead stretched a paw to touch the bowl in her hand. Mari laughed and gave him a few more bites.

After finishing her bowl, she returned to the common area to clean up. Then, returning to her room, she opened a bottle of cider. Mari glanced at her phone. Detective Booker hadn't returned her call. He must be off for the weekend.

The sabotage of her car bothered her. Who would do that and why? She hoped it wasn't Felicity Kent. She had seen her in Oak Harbor. Why would she sabotage her car? They had had a lovely conversation yesterday and today. She seemed friendly, and Mari didn't think she was obvious searching for clues about the murder. No one knew about the flash drive except for Heather, or so she thought. She felt she was still in the dark about solving the murder. Still, nothing made sense.

And then she felt the lump in her pocket. Did the killer think or know she had the flash drive? How could they?

And she still needed to talk with Joe and find out why he was so moody. Mari longed to speak with one of her family. She didn't want to worry them and knew they would pick up on her anxiety about the murder. Her mom would freak out if she found out about her car being sabotaged. She would probably tell her to leave Meadowood immediately and to come home. That's something Mari would never do. Her sister Violet was a nut about mysteries. She would be the one to talk with. But, if she talked with Violet, Violet would snitch to her parents. Her brother Bob would be someone to talk with…maybe. And now it was too late to talk to Grandad and Nan. They would be asleep. Mari sighed. She was still in a rut and no closer to solving the murder. But someone thought she was. She wished she had the same confidence. Actually, no, she didn't!

She needed something to stop her swirling head. Mari got ready for bed. She pulled out her plant propagation textbook. It was certainly dry enough to put her to sleep. She thought she would finish a few chapters and read until she fell asleep.

After falling asleep so early, Mari woke up just after

dawn. She tiptoed downstairs to make coffee, not wanting to make noise for her housemates. She was shocked to see Joe at the kitchen island on his laptop.

"Hi, Joe," she greeted. "You're up early."

"I have work to catch up on," he said morosely.

"Work? You didn't get your assignments in?"

She brewed her coffee and sat down near him.

He sighed audibly.

"I'm ADHD. I was just diagnosed. School has always been difficult for me. I am an aural learner, meaning I can excel at hearing lectures. I'm good with hands-on stuff, but reading escapes me. Writing has always been a challenge. Staying on a task long enough to finish it has always been hard. Most people don't understand that sometimes choosing how to complete something paralyzes me. And, then, I don't get things done. No one knows this, but I was in this program last year and needed to drop out. They let me back in again, but it's not working well."

"Don't they have accommodations for you?"

"They do, but they only help to a point. I'm still struggling."

"Geez, Joe. I had no idea."

"Yeah, I need to trick myself into getting things done. The smallest thing can be distracting. I exercise a lot to keep my brain focused. And I can't take the medication before you ask." But he flashed her a smile. "Thanks for creating those flashcards. They're terrific. I just wish there were a version with audio."

"That wouldn't be too difficult to produce. I think it could even be created in a PowerPoint, Joe."

His eyes brightened. "Really?"

"Well, I don't want to make any promises, but I will check it out. Today, probably."

They were both quiet for a few minutes. She sipped her coffee.

Finally, she asked, "Is that why you changed? You seemed so happy-go-lucky the first week."

"Yeah, I slid right back into the hole from a year ago. Fuller and Knight are great people, but they're old school. And Meadowood isn't a college, not really. It's associated with Eastern Shore University, but they seem to run their own game."

"Well, they need to get a grip. I like them very much, but they must bend a little if you want to stay in the program. This would be bad for Meadowood's reputation."

"There have been other students that haven't made it through the program. It's not considered Meadowood's fault."

"What? They don't understand what's going on with your brain?"

"I don't think so. I haven't won any points since I've been here. First, Meadowood wants students who will be shining stars in botany. I keep thinking they want to see me behind one of their lawnmowers."

"Joe! That's a terrible thing to say."

He shrugged. "I'm keeping my head down and doing my best."

Mari laughed, "My mom would say you got an "A" for effort." And then, she changed the subject. "What's your focus, Joe?"

"Woodland plants. Meadowood has one of the best woodland gardens in the United States."

"The Woodland Path is one of my favorite gardens. And we're lucky to have Dr. Fuller and her tree expertise at Meadowood. Franklin came here to study under her," Mari shared.

She was suddenly inspired. "Have you met Boothby?"

"Who?"

"The old gardener that lives in the cottage by the Woodland Walk. He's been a Meadowood institution for years."

"The old guy?"

Mari smiled, "Yup, that's him. He's terrific."

Joe shook his head, "No, I haven't met him."

"Look, you finish up your work. I'll bake up something quick, and we can walk over to his cottage in a while."

"Are you sure?"

"Sure, I'm sure. If you have any questions about the work, I'll be right here while I pull together this coffee cake thing. I think, at least. Let me find a recipe."

She scrolled through her phone and found a one-bowl coffeecake recipe.

Joe worked, and Mari baked. He asked her a couple of questions but remained silent for the most part.

When the coffee cake was done, Mari wrapped it in a towel to stay warm. Joe closed his laptop and ran it up to his room. Joe offered to carry the coffee cake as they left.

Mari showed Joe the way to Boothby's cottage.

"What do you think about this murder business?" she asked.

Joe shrugged, "To be honest, I've been so caught up in my own problems I haven't given it much thought."

"Did you know Dr. Wellington?"

"Nah."

"And, what do you think about Dr. Knight's letter opener being the murder weapon?"

"Look, I don't have any love for Dr. Knight. I don't think he could stab someone. It's not in his personality, and he's not strong enough. The guy is ancient!"

"Just wait until you meet Boothby. Now *he's* ancient."

Mari rang the bell outside the gate at Boothby's cottage. They waited. Mari rang it again. Maybe he wasn't home. She rang the bell a third time, wondering if he was in the forest playing the woodland flute he owned. But then, she heard footsteps.

"Mari! What a lovely surprise! Come in. Come in."

Boothby opened the gate for them.

"And, who's this?" Mari introduced Joe and handed Boothby the coffee cake.

"Oh, how kind of you, Mari. You must both pop in for a spot of tea. That's how Artie would say it, eh?"

When they settled around Boothby's kitchen table, Mari told him that Joe focused on woodland plants. She offered to make tea while they talked. Boothby and Joe hit it off, trading favorite plant varieties and discussing them. Mari made the tea and cut the cake. They enjoyed the tea and cake and discussed plants, and Boothby shared stories about the Woodland Walk gardens and how they had changed over the years. After she finished her cup of tea, Mari excused herself.

"I'm sorry I need to go so soon," she explained to Boothby, "but I promised a friend I would try to help him with his project." She turned and winked at Joe. "I'll see you soon," and she gave the old man a peck on the cheek. "See you later, Joe. Be sure to share Boothby's 'pearls of wisdom' with me later."

Mari went back to the dorm and ensconced herself in her room. She researched how to add voice narration to a PowerPoint presentation. It wasn't hard. She imported the flashcards and worked on a voice-over. It took her the bulk of the day, but it kept her busy and her mind off the murder. She finished it and sent the file to Joe.

"Well, Nepeta, we've done our good deeds for the day."

Nepeta yawned in response.

"I wonder what our friend Heather is up to," she told the cat as she fished her phone out of her pocket and texted Heather.

Heather texted that she would be right over; moments later, there was a knock.

"Hey, girlfriend," Heather greeted. "Have you been enjoying this relaxing Sunday? I have been a sloth because I know there's a lot of work ahead."

Mari filled her in on Joe, making the coffee cake, visiting Boothby, and working on the PowerPoint presentation for Joe.

"Joe's not the killer," Mari stated firmly.

"It doesn't sound like it. So, where are we on things? Felicity Kent, for sure. But, I'm going to play the devil's advocate here. What if it was Dr. Knight?" She held up her hand to stop Mari from speaking and said, "Hear me out. The evidence is there, Mari. His cane tracks were near the Clock Tower. He admits to being there the night of the murder. Yes, he's a frail old man, but what happens when the adrenaline kicks in? Wellington was obviously a pompous ass. I can imagine him bringing up the past and taunting Dr. Knight. That would make anyone crazy. And it's Dr. Knight's letter opener. You admitted he's a King Arthur nut. Maybe he carries it around. Who knows?"

Mari was silent. She didn't like it, but Heather made sense. "So, two suspects for the murder? Do you think the police come for Dr. Knight again? I don't know why it's been so quiet on the police end. We have a murderer running around."

"Who knows? And Meadowood is probably keeping as much as possible quiet, not only to the public but also to us."

CHAPTER FIFTEEN

Mari was morose the next day. Heather went on at great length about how Dr. Knight could be the murderer. Guilt ate at her for doubting her Grandad's opinion of Dr. Knight and for doubting Dr. Knight, too. She wasn't sure she could look him in the eye.

There had been no word from Detective Booker. She was puzzled by this, but conceded detectives also had a right to a weekend. She hoped he would call today. If not, she would call again.

"Hi, Mari," Ren greeted her downstairs. Once again, she had woken early, but Ren was sitting in the spot that Joe had sat in the previous day.

"Are you all right?" He asked with genuine concern in his voice.

Mari shook her head. "No, I don't think so." She busied herself making coffee and then sat by Ren. "It's this murder business," she sighed. "I can't figure it out."

"Uh, you're not supposed to," Ren said. "That's the job for the police."

"I know, but they seem stumped as well. Heather convinced me it could be Dr. Knight last night, and I don't want to believe it."

"He had a motive. Albeit old, but those old wounds fester. He was there, too."

"I know, I know."

"I wonder if he'll be in class today."

"Your guess is as good as mine. I hope so. I like learning about the Meadowood Cultivars."

"Me too. That's a field I'm interested in. I want to save endangered plants and give them new life in a botanical garden. I've been interested in plant hunting all my life. It was quite ruthless, you know, back in the day. You probably know the story of the black tulip. Thousands of plants need to be saved."

"That's pretty cool."

"And, I could return to Korea. There's a fast-growing trend in selling rare plants. In Korea, people are making a lot of money raising and selling rare plants. It's a huge online business."

"Really?"

Ren nodded.

"It's nice you have it all worked out. I'm still floundering on what I want to do. Garden design attracts me. Working at Meadowood or another botanic garden and planning the exhibits would be nice."

Her phone rang, and Mari jumped in surprise. It was Detective Booker's number showing on the phone.

"Excuse me, it's the police. I had better take this."

Mari answered as she stepped outside into the morning. She walked to the Labyrinth area to speak. Nepeta followed her and started chasing a butterfly. She tried not to laugh, but to greet the Detective instead.

"Detective Booker, hello!"

"Hi, Ms. Saille. I'm sorry to get back to you so late. You said you found something by the Clock Tower?"

"Yes, it was a flash drive. I didn't look at the files but thought it might be important."

"It could be. We're planning on being at the gardens later this morning. Can I pick it up then?"

"Sure. Also, one more thing. I don't know if it's connected to the murder or not, but my car was sabotaged. I almost had an accident on Saturday. The guy at the automotive shop was pretty sure it was deliberate."

"Not good. Are you poking around in this case?"

"I, uh, sort of, I guess? I didn't think I was being obvious."

"Maybe not to you, but to a killer that could be discovered, they're probably paranoid. You could be in grave danger. Does anyone else know you have the flash drive?"

"Only Heather Arum."

She heard an audible sigh.

"I'll see you soon." He hung up.

Mari stared at her phone. What did that mean? Exasperated, she returned to the kitchen. Ren was still at the end of the kitchen island. He was looking at something on his phone.

He looked up. "Well?"

She shrugged, "Detective Booker said he would be here later today. I don't know what to make of it."

She pulled granola from the cupboard and fruit and yogurt from the refrigerator. Heather came down, and she offered to make her a bowl.

"What's wrong? Still bothered about our discussion?"

"Yes," Mari admitted. "And Detective Booker called. He said the police will be here later today."

Heather's eyebrows raised into her coppery curls.

"Did he say why? Did you tell him what you found?"

Mari gave her a warning look as people filled the common area, getting breakfast and going to the potting shed.

"Sorry," Heather whispered, "I don't think anyone heard." Mari nodded and concentrated on eating.

"Now that Dr. Knight's back, maybe we'll have a normal week," Nichelle commented.

"Don't count on it," Peter drawled. "They need to get the murder solved before normalcy reigns again."

"And, what's normal?" Sunny stated. "We're all new to this program, so we don't know what normal is, right?"

Mari looked quickly at Joe, who froze on his way into the kitchen at Sunny's announcement. He took a breath, smiled at Mari, and made breakfast.

They left en masse for the Potting Shed, where an extremely frustrated-looking Dr. Fuller awaited them. She seemed to be clutching her coffee this morning and not drinking it reverently, as usual.

"Good morning, saplings," she drawled, "I was hoping for a normal week this week in our program, but that is not to be had. The police contacted us much too early this morning. They are returning to Meadowood to question everyone again. I will provide the detectives with a list of your cell phone numbers. When they call you, please be prompt and make your way to the classroom area as requested. In light of this development, the class will be canceled today." She put the word development in air quotes.

"I spoke with Dr. Knight. We will assign you a research task as you work in your assigned area. As you clean and prune your assigned area, think about future acquisitions to your area. Research, write about your findings, and write a convincing, persuasive essay, including a budget, to be completed and submitted by midnight Sunday night. You will be assigned to your area for the entire week. I would suggest that you make a list of the current plantings. Make sure you also write about what plantings you might choose to remove and why. It will be your choice in your project if you add and subtract a few plants or completely overhaul the garden. You will have access to the archives and previous plantings in the garden areas. Keep that in mind if you are assigned to a historical portion of the property. Be sensitive to the history of Meadowood and budget, even though this is a 'pie in the sky' sort of project. Remember, you are here for public garden administration training. Renovating gardens is something you'll likely do as a public garden administrator."

Dr. Fuller paused and took a sip of coffee. "Any questions?" She waited. None came.

"Franklin, you are assigned to the Northern end of the Woodland Walk. Joe, the Southern end."

The men fist-bumped.

Dr. Fuller continued, "Ren, the Celtic Knot garden. Heather, you'll be working at the Meadow Garden. Nichelle, you'll work in the Formal French Gardens and Sunny, the Sensory Gardens. Peter, please consider the plantings around the Blackthorn Mansion. And, Mari, the outside of the Conservatory."

They all looked happy but exhibited 'deer in the headlights' looks.

"Saplings! Go!"

They left, chattering excitedly. Everyone seemed happy with their assignments except Ren.

"I think I have the most boring garden on site," he complained.

"Really? I think just the opposite. Think of how you

can make plays on puzzles and time with plants. Like the Monkey Puzzle Tree or the different varieties of Thyme. Maybe something Celtic, since it's a Celtic Knot Garden. What about "The Bells of Ireland" plants? It's not exciting to look at, but it would provide nice layering and a vertical touch if you have different thymes."

"Wanna trade?" Ren asked with a sarcastic edge to his voice, "But truly, thanks, you're getting my mind working on the project."

Mari laughed, "Good. I'm considering the plants that were used when many of the Victorian Glass Houses were built. It would be nice to add a little history."

"I can see you up late researching."

"And, spending time in the Meadowood research library. I haven't had a chance to explore it yet."

Everyone went their separate ways outside. Mari waved to Heather. She knew she was excited about the Meadow project, Heather, and her love of insects. She would most likely make sure host plantings were in place for a variety of beneficial insects.

Mari stepped back and studied the Conservatory. Near the conservatory's walls were a number of understory trees and bushes, followed by bushes and smaller plantings that were a mixture of annuals and perennials. She didn't have a clue as to what plantings were Victorian or not. First things first, she would need to make a list. She pulled out her notebook and drew the Conservatory's rough outline. Mari outlined each Conservatory wall on the ensuing pages, marking them as North, South, East, and West. Starting at the Northern edge, she crawled into the garden and listed the current plants. She was halfway through the Northern side's garden when her phone rang. It was Detective Booker. She wasn't surprised.

"Hello. Miss Saille? It's Detective Booker. Can you

come to be interviewed and bring the flash drive?"

"Yes, of course. I'm at the Conservatory. I'll be there in a few moments."

She stowed her notebook and pen in her backpack and went to the Visitors' Center. Detective Booker stood outside the classroom door with his feet spread apart, looking like he took the at-ease military stance. He smiled at her and motioned for her to come inside. Detective Parker was already seated. He always made her nervous, and her hands started to sweat. She felt grimy from crawling in the bushes while looking for their tags. She brushed her damp hands over her khakis and removed her hat, praying her curly, strawberry-blonde hair wasn't sticking up everywhere.

"Ms. Saille," Detective Parker greeted.

He pronounced her name as "sail – lee." She gritted her teeth.

"Good morning," she forced herself to say.

Detective Parker held a chair for her to sit down and she flashed him a nervous smile and said thank you.

"Detective Booker tells me you found something at the Clock Tower garden area."

"Yes, sir. I was assigned to weed around the Clock Tower area. I spied this," and she dug in her pocket to pull out the flash drive. "At first, I thought it was a piece of mulch, but I picked it up by the edges to give to you."

"And where has it been since you picked it up?"

"I've kept it in my pocket, sir."

"Effectively rubbing any fingerprints off as you moved around," he said in disgust.

"Oh! I'm sorry, I didn't think of that."

"It's okay, Ms. Saille," Detective Booker soothed.

He pronounced her name correctly. She smiled at him.

"Where at the Clock Tower did you find this?"

"Near where Dr. Wellington's body was. It looks like it flew out of his hand or pocket when he fell."

"Conjecture," Detective Parker snapped.

"Okay," Mari said evenly. Inside, she was beginning to get a little steamed.

"Did you put it in your computer?"

"No, sir."

"And who did you tell about the flash drive?"

"Only Heather Arum, another graduate student here."

"Hmm…and Detective Booker said your car was sabotaged?"

"Yes, sir. That is according to the mechanic at the automotive repair place in Oak Harbor. I have his card in my room."

"Do you have anything else to add?"

"Well, sir. I don't think Felicity Kent murdered Dr. Wellington. I don't know, of course," she was beginning to babble because she was nervous. "She, one of the Meadowood Fellows, knows, that is, knew, Dr. Wellington. His actions made her lose her job as a faculty member in Britain. She knows Dr. Knight, too."

"Yes, we've been looking into that," Detective Booker informed.

"But, she seems so nice. I had tea with her the other day. She was in Oak Harbor at the Farmers Market on Saturday when Heather and I were there."

"So, she was in the vicinity when your car was sabotaged?"

"Yes, sir. But how could she get a large nail into my tire? I would think she would have to be pretty strong to do that!"

"You leave the whys up to us to figure out," Detective Parker intoned. "You need to stop snooping."

"Yes, sir. But I wasn't *really* snooping."

"Really?"

Mari sat uncomfortably in her chair.

"Didn't you want to exonerate Dr. Knight?"

She looked at her hands twisted in her lap and nodded.

"That's all for now, Ms. Saille."

She stood to go. Detective Booker had a worried look. "Be careful, Ms. Saille."

She nodded and turned to go. She heard Detective Booker say, "This case is something. There are so many players, but everyone seems to have a perfectly good alibi."

"Somebody killed Dr. Wellington. I aim to find out who," she heard Detective Parker state.

At least he wanted to get to the bottom of things. He mentioned they were looking at Felicity Kent.

Mairi looked at the crowded Visitors' Center. A couple of busloads of people had come in. She felt bad for the employees at the entrance gate, the café, and the gift shop. The visitors crowded the areas. She glanced at the time on her phone. she had time to go back, grab an early lunch, get her laptop, and go to the research library for this project.

Back at the dorm, the front door was ajar. They had strict orders to keep things locked up due to the tourists. No one seemed to be about. She stopped and listened. The old building was soundly built, and she couldn't hear anything. She went upstairs to her room. Her door wasn't closed. She was sure she locked it this morning. She pushed at the door gently. It swung open to reveal her room, usually fairly neat, but now looked like a tornado had attacked it. Clothes were out of the bureau and closets, and cushions were off the chairs. Even the mattress was askew. With shaky hands, she dialed Detective

Booker.

He answered on the first ring, and she explained what had happened.

"Don't touch anything," he warned. "Go downstairs and outside. Don't touch the door handles. Wait outside the door. Don't let anyone go in. I will be right there."

Mari went down the stairs as fast as she could. She used the hem of her Meadowood shirt to open the door. She went to sit on a bench that was adjacent to the doorway. Nervously, she looked around while waiting for Detective Booker.

Nepeta approached Mari, meowed loudly, and jumped into her lap. Mari hugged the cat fiercely, telling herself not to cry.

Ren and Sunny came up the path. They were chatting about the project.

"We can't go inside," she told them when they reached her.

"Can't go inside? Why?" Ren asked.

"Somebody ransacked my room. The police are on the way. The front door was open too when I got here."

"Oh, my! You poor thing!" Sunny cried. She sat down next to Mari and put a hand on her arm. She petted Nepeta with her other hand.

The other students came along, too, as it was lunchtime. Everyone gathered around Mari and peppered her with questions. Heather was the last to arrive, and she was with Detective Booker. She must have been in the interview with him when Mari called.

Dr. Fuller came up the path, hurrying along and a little out of breath.

"What's going on?" she demanded.

"When I returned to the dorm, I found the front door open and my room ransacked," Mari told her evenly. "I called Detective Booker. He asked me to wait outside."

"I've called the Forensic team. They should be here in a few minutes," Detective Booker informed everyone.

"Were the other rooms ransacked?" someone asked.

"I don't know yet. When the team comes, we'll check it out. In the meantime, you can't enter the dormitory."

"What about lunch?" Peter groused, "My food and my wallet are inside."

"Everyone can go to the café. We'll charge it to the department," Dr. Fuller offered.

"But Mari needs to stay here. I have questions and may have more when we get inside. Can someone bring her something?" Detective Booker asked.

"I can," Heather volunteered.

"Good."

"Can we get you anything, Detective Booker?" Dr. Fuller offered.

"Thank you, no."

The group left, and Detective Booker sat next to Mari as they waited for the Forensic team. Nepeta left Mari's lap, bumped his head against Detective Booker's chin, and purred. He laughed and petted the cat.

"How are you doing?" he asked Mari.

"Okay," she said, not too convincingly, with her smile on the watery edge. "It's scary, you know? It makes everything too real."

He nodded.

"Do you think you were targeted?"

She shrugged. "How or why?"

"The flash drive," he said gently.

"Who knew? I mean, I'm sure it wasn't Heather. Is someone watching me? Why? I just found the body."

"And the flash drive."

"That's creepy," she said and shivered.

"Yes, it is. Until we resolve this, you must always be with someone. I don't want to remove you from the area or the case, but do you have a safe place to go if you need to?"

"Home. It's north of here, a little more than an hour at the top of the bay. I'd rather see Grandad and Nan in the UK. My mom would fuss too much."

Detective Booker laughed, "That's a little too far."

The forensic team arrived and went to work. They dusted for prints on the door. When they cleared the common area, Detective Booker asked Mari to come inside and wait on the couch.

"Stay here," he ordered.

Mari stayed with Nepeta, purring on her lap.

CHAPTER SIXTEEN

Mari tried to wait patiently with Nepeta but found herself tapping her foot. She texted Heather, *they're upstairs. I'm in the common area. Waiting…*

She texted back, *Be there soon with lunch.*

Mari returned with a happy face emoji.

About five minutes later, Heather came carrying a to-go box. Inside was one of the spicy chickpea wraps.

"Aww, thank you, Heather. I am really not hungry. I'm a little freaked out by all this."

"I can understand that. Everyone was asking a lot of questions in the cafeteria. I didn't say anything about the flash drive or suspicions."

"Thanks."

Detective Booker came downstairs, "Ms. Saille, can you come to your room?"

Mari and Heather followed the detective upstairs. Heather gasped when she saw the destruction, and Mari just stood. In addition to the destruction, fingerprint powder coated nearly everything.

"Um, you can start to clean up, but you might want to sleep somewhere else tonight."

"She can bunk in with me. I think there's a roll-away cot somewhere for guests. We can put it in my room.

"Did you find anything?" Mari asked.

"We'll have to wait for prints to get back. Do you see anything missing?"

Mari looked around her room. It looked like things had been dumped and strewn about, but everything was still there, or so she thought.

"I'll have to let you know as I put things back, but it doesn't look like it. It looks like they just tossed stuff around looking for something," she told Detective Booker.

"Fair enough. If you have some time now, I can help you a bit. We can get your room mostly together between the three of us."

Mari looked at Heather. "I guess so," she agreed. "Heather?"

Heather nodded, "Let's do it. Mari, you should work on the bureau. Detective, can you help me get the mattress on the bed? You can pick up the books and stuff, and I'll deal with the closet."

"If you have a vacuum, that's the best way to clean up this powder. Getting it wet only makes more of a mess."

Heather went to get the communal vacuum from a closet down the hall. Mari stood, looking in shock at everything in disarray. Once the cushions were back in place, and the bed made, it started to look more normal. Mari refolded and put things back in the bureau. Heather worked on the closet. Detective Booker ran the vacuum sucking up all the fingerprint dust.

They worked for an hour, and Mari asked to stop.

"I can't do any more today. I – I," and she burst into

tears.

Heather came over to hug her. Detective Booker patted her on the back.

"Why me? I don't understand."

"Another piece we need to put in place with this murder investigation. I still think the murderer knew you had the flash drive. We'll get to work on that."

"With this project due in a week, I'm glad they left your laptop," she said with relief.

"You're not kidding. I was planning on going to the library here at Meadowood this afternoon. Now I'm behind a day, and you are too. I'm sorry, Heather."

"It's okay, my friend. We'll figure it out."

"I think you are in shock, tired, and hungry. Your stomach is growling, and you didn't eat lunch. Why don't I run to Oak Harbor and pick up sandwiches? You guys can finish putting stuff back and clearing off some of the icky powder."

Mari put her head in her hand, "And find Nepeta, please?"

"Done. Detective, what can I bring you from the sandwich shop?"

Heather made notes on her phone when Detective Booker and Mari told her their choices and called in the order. Within a few minutes, she went downstairs and brought a squirming cat to Mari's room.

"Nepeta!" Mari cried happily when Heather put Nepeta on the floor.

"He's not happy with me. He was stuck outside the dorm, meowing to get in."

Nepeta sniffed around the room and then jumped onto his favorite spot on the window seat. He started to wash himself, ignoring the humans.

"I'm heading out to pick up sandwiches. I'll be back

soon."

"Where does this go?" Detective Booker pointed to the vacuum.

"In the closet, down the hall, I can put it back."

"Let me," he insisted.

Mari plopped onto the window seat with Nepeta. He touched his nose to hers and licked it. She tried not to start crying again.

"This is pretty crazy, Nepeta," she whispered into his fur.

Nepeta responded with a soft meow and then started to purr. Detective Booker returned to the room and sat in the small upholstered chair near the window seat. He looked overly large in it, his body and legs much too large for the petite chair. Mari tried not to laugh and buried her face in Nepeta's fur for a minute.

"How does it look now?"

Mari scanned the room. "Much better than an hour ago." She shivered. "Were the locks broken?"

"Looks like they had lock-picking tools. Anyone can buy those at a local tool store. They weren't professional, I don't think. There was some damage. Dr. Fuller said the maintenance guys would be here soon."

Mari shivered, "I think I'm going to have nightmares."

"So, I suggest you take Heather's offer and sleep in her room tonight and maybe the next few nights."

Mari felt defeated and depleted. "I guess so." She felt at a loss for words.

Detective Booker cleared his throat, "I'm sorry I didn't respond to your phone call. That's my work phone, and I was at a friend's wedding. I took a red-eye home. I need to give you the police station's and my personal cell number."

"Oh," Mari responded quietly, paused, and pulled

out her phone. "Thanks."

"You must be really tired," she said, realization dawning.

"I am. It was quite the weekend. I was able to snag a couple of hours of sleep on the way home, but airplane sleep isn't the same as being in your own bed."

"That's for sure. We always fly at night when we visit Nan and Grandad, but it's exhausting. I usually crawl into bed for a nap when we arrive. It's probably the time change, too. I don't like getting so scrunched up in the airplane seats. I always look longingly at those First Class or Business Class people with those bed-like seats, blankets, and pillows. My parents take five of us over, so it's economy for us."

He nodded and looked like he wanted to say something, but Heather burst in the door with a large paper bag. A potato chip bag rustled and peeked out of the top.

"Dinner," she announced. She looked around, "Wow, it looks almost like it's back to normal. The maintenance guy is downstairs. He said he would be up in a few minutes. He's changing the lock to the dormitory, complaining of all the keys he needed to make."

"Thanks, Heather. This hits the spot."

Detective Booker followed with his thanks but was trying to keep a mooching Nepeta away from his sandwich. Finally, he tore off a piece of meat and cheese and put it on the floor. The cat attacked it and then looked for more.

"You would think he was starving. He's not," she nodded to the full bowl of kibble near the bathroom door.

The maintenance man, with "Tom" embroidered on his shirt, came to the door and knocked. He nodded in their direction and greeted them, "Evening. I'll get this done in a jiffy."

They watched as the maintenance man removed the old lock and replaced it with a new one. It was done in under ten minutes. He came inside the room with the key. He spied Nepeta.

"That cat! He's a mooch. He's constantly hanging out at our building."

"He likes it here."

"Yeah, he's spoiled," Tom commented and shook his head. Here's your key for this door and the key for the front door. I need you to initial that you received it."

Mari did so.

"And now I need to get new keys to everyone in the building." He mildly complained and then looked at Heather, "You picked yours up downstairs, right?"

"Yes," Heather responded. "I can walk you to the other rooms. Let me know who needs keys."

She left with Tom after Mari said thank you.

"I'll wait until Heather returns, and then I'll be leaving too," Detective Booker told her.

"Oh, okay," Mari said, not really wanting him to leave. Then, a realization dawned on her: "Detective Booker, you said you don't want me to be alone for a while. That's not possible during the day. We're all assigned to different parts of the garden. I'm at the Conservatory. Heather is at the northern end with the Meadow Garden. We're everywhere for the entire week as we have a big project due."

"Hmm, that's a bit of a problem. What time do you start your day?"

"Seven-thirty."

"I'll be here."

"What?"

"I can't take a uniform and change his or her duty. We're short-staffed as it is. I'll clear it with Detective

Parker. Don't worry."

"Okay," Mari responded. "I need to get a list of the plants outside the Conservatory and also go to the Library for research."

He nodded. "I'll bring my laptop, too. It will work out. The break-in and vandalism here put a crimp in the works. We want to check out that flash drive, hopefully tomorrow. We have a lot of fingerprints to process and notes to pull together. I believe Detective Parker is interviewing Ms. Kent."

Heather burst into the room, announcing, "All done."

Detective Booker stood, "And, that's my cue to go. Until tomorrow, then."

Behind Detective Booker, Heather's eyebrows shot up into her auburn bangs. Mari ignored her.

"Thank you, Detective Booker, for everything. See you in the morning," Mari added.

Heather's eyebrows descended as Detective Booker turned around and thanked Heather for dinner.

"No problem."

He left, and Heather shut Mari's door firmly and said in a stage whisper, "What was that all about? Until tomorrow? Are we in a romantic movie? Where's your Regency dress?"

Mari couldn't help it. She was punch-drunk on stress. She doubled over, laughing. It took her a minute to get herself together.

"You heard him; he doesn't want me going anywhere alone. We're scattered throughout the garden with this project, so he's coming to babysit me."

"Nice!"

"I guess. I hope I can concentrate on the project."

"And, not look into his dreamy eyes?" Heather teased.

"Oh, Heather. Be serious."

"I am. Does he really think it could be dangerous?"

"I guess, especially after today's ransacking." She shivered visibly.

"Well, I agree with him that you shouldn't sleep alone. Let's find that fold-out cot and set it up in my room."

Mari looked around her room. "What about Nepeta?"

"He can come too."

"Deal."

They scrounged around until they found the fold-out cot tucked away in a storage closet. Together, they wheeled the thing to Heather's room and set it up.

"I'll go back and get ready for bed, get sheets, and Nepeta. I think I'm safe in the dorm with everyone here."

"Okay, text me if you need me."

Mari returned to her room. It felt strange to go to Heather's. She showered and pulled out things she needed for Heather's and tomorrow. She made another trip with Nepeta's litterbox and food dishes. Lastly, she brought Nepeta, who was not happy being taken from her room. Once she was settled on the cot, he tromped all over her and settled in her lap. She petted him absently, glad he was there.

"Heather," she said finally, "This isn't making sense. I can't figure out why anyone would ransack my room unless they knew about the flash drive. And how did they find out about it?"

"I promise I didn't say anything to anyone," Heather assured her.

"So, it still comes down to Felicity Kent and Dr. Knight. I still can't see Dr. Knight murdering anyone, but I confess, I don't know him well. It's all from what Grandad has said. I can't see him sabotaging my car. And,

Felicity Kent, I mean, what's her story? She seemed so nice. She was in town when we were there, and my tire was sabotaged."

"And, she could sneak here from the Fellows housing," Heather added.

"Hmm. Maybe. Maybe I'll bring it up since I'll be with Detective Booker all day."

"I think you should. And, hey, why didn't he call you back this weekend?"

"Oh, that…I called his work phone. He was out of town at a wedding. He gave me the station number and his personal cell."

"Whoa. That's interesting."

"I guess."

They continued to talk, but Mari's stress of the day was catching up with her. She yawned. Nepeta was purring a lullaby. She found herself dozing and waking until Heather laughed at her.

"I'll be quiet. You need sleep."

"Night," Mari said faintly, and she didn't remember anything until morning.

CHAPTER
SEVENTEEN

Mari hurried back to her room the next morning to change and pack her laptop and notebook into a bag. She hadn't had the chance to begin her research and felt a little behind. She wondered what this day would bring. It would be odd to have Detective Booker tagging along with her.

He arrived promptly at seven-fifteen, large coffee in hand. The group of students was surprised to see him there. Mari was finishing her granola, yogurt, and berries.

"I need to clean up quickly, and then I'll be ready," she told him.

"And you can relax a little. We're not meeting with Dr. Fuller this morning. We're on our own," Peter drawled.

"That's true," Mari agreed. "I want to get the plants written down that are currently around the Conservatory. I missed a half day yesterday and need to catch up."

"Boothby might be able to help you on the historic part. He's been at Meadowood for over fifty years. His stories are tremendous. He's seen it all here," Joe commented.

"Good idea, Joe," Mari said and flashed him a smile.

She cleaned her dishes and turned to Detective Booker, "Ready."

They walked outside, with Nepeta following. Mari led Detective Booker through the Celtic Knot Labyrinth. Nepeta became distracted and started playing with lavender blossoms hanging low.

Mari laughed, "He's such a cat. He's so silly sometimes."

"You're definitely his human."

"Then, I'm really lucky."

"This place is something else. You're so lucky to wake up to this every day."

"Trust me, I know. It's been a life-long dream to be here."

"I'm a history buff. I grew up in a small town outside of Gettysburg. I remember reading about Lord Blackthorn and his shipping industry. He was pretty important during the Civil War. I can't believe I'm walking where he walked and seeing what he saw. It's pretty cool. I'll have to tell my uncle. He's a Civil War fanatic! He's one of those guys that does the reenactment battles."

"Have you done that too?"

"Guilty. When I was younger, I was one of the drummer boys in the Union Army—had the costume and everything. I didn't stick with it, though. Once you're dead in one of the battles, you have to just lie still until the battle is over. It wasn't much fun."

"I can only imagine if you were ten and you had to lie still for a long time."

They reached the Conservatory, and Mari went to the Southern side. She put her backpack down and pulled out her notebook and pen. She told Detective

Booker about their plant acquisition project and all that it entailed with the history, budget, and current plantings.

"Is there any way I can help? That's a lot of work."

"Sure, I guess so. I'm reading the plant labels and writing them down. I did the Northern side yesterday morning. I need to complete the South, East, and Western sides."

"Where are the plant labels?"

"Look for something on a stake near the plant; for bushes and trees, there's a copper label attached to a wire."

"Got it." Detective Booker took a notebook and pen from his backpack. "I'll start in the middle and work towards you. That way, you'll be fairly close by."

"Okay." She wanted to roll her eyes but refrained, secretly pleased he was close.

It was a beautiful late spring day. Mari got into her zone of being around the plants and finding the labels. The evergreens were fairly large, and she wondered how old they were. They obstructed the view of the conservatory's architecture. She stood back, considering smaller plantings that would somehow enhance the historic building. She met Detective Booker in the middle and copied his findings onto her scrawled map.

They repeated their routine before moving to the eastern side. The Conservatory was an imposing site covering more than fifteen acres. It took them the remainder of the morning to log the plants.

"Lunch?" he asked when they had completed the plant inventory.

"Sure. I can make us some tuna or egg salad," she offered.

"What if I take you to lunch at the Café. You got dinner last night."

"Um, that was Heather."

"Okay, I owe her lunch. Humor me, okay?"

"Okay."

Mari enjoyed spending time with Detective Booker. As they worked on the inventory about Meadowood and the plants, he asked a lot of questions. He didn't seem disturbed that she didn't have all the answers. He seemed genuinely interested in the history of Meadowood. She felt relaxed and safe around him, and honestly, she had a few butterflies in her stomach when he looked at her a certain way.

During their lunch, he shared more about growing up in rural Pennsylvania and Mari shared her time growing up on the Northern portion of the Chesapeake Bay. He asked her about her grandparents in Britain. She was sad to see their lunch come to an end. They both seemed hesitant to leave the patio of the Café. It was a lovely spot that looked out over Blackthorn Cove and the bay beyond.

"What's next on the agenda?" he asked.

"The Library. I need to research the historical plantings around the Conservatory. Do you really think it's necessary for me to have an escort everywhere?"

"I do. This murderer has been unpredictable. For an unknown reason, he or she is now targeting you. I think he or she is paranoid. It's called persecutory delusions. The murderer may feel that since you found the victim and have been asking questions. There's a high rate of murders where the murderer feels they are defending themselves. And the situation has escalated by the trashing of your room. I don't have the information yet on what's on that flash drive. I know we are working on the fingerprints."

"Okay. I guess it's off to the library for the afternoon

then."

They bussed their table and went upstairs in the Visitors Center. The library was past the classrooms and offices. It wasn't a large library, and Mari hoped it had some information for her. The librarian was very helpful and pulled out volumes with older photographs of Meadowood. Detective Booker was excited about the history.

"In all these photos, they seem to have these narrow evergreens. They're like those creepy Italian Cypress trees. In all the photographs, they look like dark ghosts or something."

"I think you have a personal problem with Cypresses," Mari teased. "But the older photographs don't have the tall trees. Shorter and narrower trees highlighted the architecture."

"You're right. Most of the listings of plants are for the gorgeous plantings inside the Conservatory and not the outside. In addition to the beautiful plants, they used the Conservatory to grow food for the estate. You know, the espaliered fruit trees that grow against the walls, plus citrus. If you want to walk through the Conservatory sometime, I can point out the historical elements."

"I would like that."

"But, for my project, I think I would like to remove the larger bushes and bring back the glory of the glass house. Maybe put those Cypress trees on each corner. They really do provide a nice, narrow vertical feature. It would be appropriate because Lord and Lady Blackthorn featured Italianate Gardens, which were in their heyday in the nineteenth century. Now, to think about the rest of the plantings."

"Sounds like you're on a roll with the project," Detective Booker said.

"I want to research other glass houses and conservatories of the time. If I can find photographs in the latter part of the nineteenth century, it should help—more research. But, I can do a lot of that on my laptop at the dorm. It's getting late."

The afternoon had passed quickly, and it was after four. The library was about to close.

"Text Heather to see if she's back."

Mari sighed. "Okay."

Heather return texted that she was indeed back at the dormitory and would take over the care and feeding of Mari. She added a smiley face emoji. She shared the text with Detective Booker.

We're on our way back, Mari texted Heather.

She thanked the librarian, and they walked back to the dorm.

"Thanks for taking care of me today."

"It wasn't a chore, Mari. I had a great time. You have an interesting life as a student here. I'll be in touch with you tomorrow about what we find. I hope we can wrap this case up."

"Me too." She shared what she and Heather had discussed last night with Detective Booker. He seemed to take it all in but didn't comment. He dropped her off at the door as Heather appeared.

"Thank you," she told him, meaning every word.

She went inside, a little sad. It had been a lovely day. Heather wanted to hear all about it, and they camped out in her room for a little while, chatting. Mari insisted she could stay in her room that night, and Heather helped her move her things and Nepeta's, too.

Nepeta hadn't greeted her at the door. She thought it was a little odd, but with the bright, sunny day, she was sure he was in a warm, bright spot in the garden. Heather asked if she wanted to go out to dinner, and Mari declined, explaining her late lunch with Detective Booker.

Mari told Heather she wanted to work on the research. She said she would be safely ensconced in her room with her laptop, and she could get dinner or whatever.

"First, a shower. That Meadow Garden was blazing hot. Even with sunblock, I have a sunburn."

Her friend did look fairly pink.

"I have some aloe lotion. Let me get it for you." Mari ran to the bathroom and rummaged in the cupboard until she found the bottle. "This will help. And take a cool shower," she advised.

"Thanks, Mom," Heather grinned and left Mari.

Mari kicked off her shoes and socks and wriggled her toes. She sat on the window seat and opened her laptop. She started researching the glass houses of the Victorian era, specifically looking for photographs of the outside. There were several articles on the popularity of glass houses and the plants inside, but she wasn't finding what she wanted in terms of plantings outside the houses. She was frustrated. How could she showcase the architecture with plantings? Perennials would be best with annuals to highlight. She would need something evergreen or at least something with year-round interest. She wracked her brain.

Her email dinged that she had an incoming message. She clicked on the icon, and the subject line was in capital letters, stating, "Nepeta News." That was odd. She clicked to open the email.

The body of the email stated, "If you want to see the cat again, come to the Clock Tower."

Nepeta! Someone had Nepeta!

She jumped up with a gasp and, not thinking, ran out the door.

CHAPTER EIGHTEEN

Who would take Nepeta? The gardens were closed, and it seemed unusually quiet. She jogged to the clock tower and was out of breath. At the door, bolt cutters, the chain, and the lock lay on the ground.

"Nepeta? Nepeta?" she shouted.

Mari heard a faint meow.

There was a decorative iron spiral stairway to the top of the clock tower. As a child, the open work filagree iron had always creeped her out, and it took her many years to have the courage to follow her older brother and sister to the top. She knew there was a room with information on the clock and doorways to the balcony.

Taking a deep breath, she went up the stairs. She didn't see anyone or any shadows. When she reached the clock room, Nepeta was in a cat carrier near the balcony railing.

"Merrow," he complained bitterly at being a prisoner.

"Nepeta! Thank goodness you're all right! Mari exclaimed as she ran out the doorway to the balcony.

"Stop right there! Not a step further!" a voice said from the doorway. Mari heard the door to the clock room shut with a thunk as the vintage hardware clicked into place, locking the door. Fear gripped her. Someone had been waiting for her on the other side of the door. She turned. When she saw the person, she was confused.

"Ren? Ren! What are you doing here?"

She noticed he had a sharp garden sickle in one hand. Her eyebrows knit together.

"Where's the flash drive, Mari? What did you do with it?"

"What?" She was confused and worried about Nepeta. Why was Ren asking about the flash drive? How did he know about it?"

"How did you know about it?"

"I overheard you and Heather talking. I have very good ears."

Mari remembered when she told Heather about the flash drive. Ren wasn't exactly close, but he was near-by. He seemed caught up in whatever he was looking at on his phone. His expression hadn't changed when they were talking. She was sure of it.

"I don't understand."

"It's not difficult, Mari. The flash drive. The one you found at the base of the Clock Tower. Where is it?" His voice was a little more forceful now. "Did you open it? Did you see what was on it? You should have. It would explain everything."

"I didn't open it, Ren. I thought it might have some-thing to do with Dr. Wellington's murder."

Ren barked a laugh.

"It's always about Dr. Wellington, isn't it? The great Dr. Wellington," he said sarcastically. "The man was a fraud. He built his life and career on lies."

"How? What happened?" Mari remembered seeing a television program about keeping a disturbed person talking. She didn't know his intent, but didn't have the flash drive. She did notice the doors to the balcony were open.

"Like Dr. Knight and countless others, he stole my research. It was research that would set me up in botany for the rest of my life! I found proof that plants could successfully stop certain kinds of cancer. It was my ticket to get into a university research position or a bio-pharmaceutical firm. *My* research, not his. He took my information and put his name on it. He was going to publish and take all the glory. And, leave me in the dust after promising." Ren stopped. He looked like he was going to cry. He swiped at his eyes before saying bitterly, "After he promised many things."

Ren looked broken. He was pale, sweating, and very angry. Now, his eyes had a cold glint in them when he looked at Mari.

"Where is it, Mari?"

"Why did you kill him, Ren?" Mari asked gently.

"It was an accident, Mari. I just wanted to threaten him, to let him know he couldn't get away with stealing my research. He thought we were coming to the tower for other reasons." he sneered. "But, when I confronted him, he made more false promises, and I became angry. I had taken Dr. Knight's letter opener. It was under a huge pile of papers on his desk. I didn't think he'd miss it, at least not at first. And I remembered I had it during our 'discussion' about my research, so I pulled it out. He started to babble, and I became angrier. I lashed out. I shoved the letter opener into his arm, and he bled out so fast. I can't believe I did that. But I can't say I'm not glad he's gone. He was a horrible man."

Mari thought quickly. "You could say it was

self-defense, Ren. Self-defense and to beat the black-mail. Right?"

"I don't know, Mari. And now, you've taken my research, too. What are you going to do with it?"

"I don't have it Ren. I don't want your research. I'm not a threat to you."

"That's what Alex said. He lied."

"Alex?"

"Dr. Alexander Wellington, Esquire. He liked to shove that title around, I can tell you."

"I'm not lying to you, Ren. I don't have your research, and I don't want it. Let Nepeta and me go. This is..." she stopped shy of saying 'crazy.'

While they were talking, she slowly walked back-ward towards Nepeta. If she could release him, he might be able to run down the stairs or at least jump onto one of the trees outside. He would be safe. She was almost there. If she faked a fall, she could land by the carrier and open it: just a step or two more.

"What now, Ren?"

"Well, if you had the flash drive, I would force you to take a swan dive off the balcony with your precious kitty in your arms. I have a nice little suicide note, too. And then, I would leave Meadowood and peddle my research to the highest bidder."

"And now?" she asked, a little afraid as he approached her.

He stopped.

"You are just a problem now, Mari. One I need to solve."

He lunged at her, wielding the razor-sharp weeder, and she did fall. Her shoulder hit the cat carrier, but she reached around and squeezed the bars to open it. Nepeta was out in a flash, growling and spitting at Ren. She grabbed him, backing further into a corner, away from Ren.

"Let us go, Ren. Please, let us go."

Nepeta was squirming, but she held on tightly. Neither Ren nor Mari noticed the sound of footsteps. Heather and Joe burst onto the balcony with a bang. Ren looked at them, confused. Joe rushed at Ren, drew back, and punched him before he could utter a word. Ren recoiled. Mari grabbed the cat carrier and swung it wildly, hitting Ren. He fell, cowering and cradling his head. Heather ran over and kicked the weeder out of his reach. They heard sirens wailing in the distance.

A few moments later, Detectives Booker and Parker arrived. Detective Parker handcuffed Ren roughly and read him his rights.

Detective Booker looked at the remaining students. "Don't move," he ordered. "We need to talk."

Mari crumbled into a ball on the floor, Nepeta in her arms. It took her a minute, but she looked up in wonder at Heather and Joe.

"I saw the email when I came to check on you," Heather explained, looking up at Joe's tall form, "And I grabbed Joe. He's the biggest of all of us. And I called the police. Apparently, they were already on their way here. You handled yourself, or should I say cat, pretty well, Mari."

"I need a minute," she told them as she tried to stand, her legs shaky.

Heather and Joe held her up on either side. They looked out at the vista of Meadowood from the top of the clock tower. Nepeta meowed.

Mari laughed. "I think he wants to go home. I do, too."

And down the stairs, they followed Nepeta all the way back to the dorm.

EPILOGUE

Mari and Nepeta collapsed onto a couch in the common area, Heather and Joe were on either side. The other students were perched on chairs or stools from the kitchen island. Sunny sat cross-legged on the floor. They waited with expectation for an explanation.

Her mind whirled with the events of the past few hours. She stroked Nepeta frequently and put her face into his fur. He was patient. He purred, and she hugged him tightly.

"This has been an unbelievable day," she began.

Tears wanted to fall, but something held them back.

"What happened?" Franklin asked. "Where's Ren?"

Joe started, "That piece of…"

Mari put a warning hand on him. To their surprise, Drs. Knight and Fuller were at the door. They came in. Nichelle and Franklin stood up and offered their seats to them. They sat.

"Apparently," Mari began, "Ren knew Dr. Wellington. Dr. Wellington stole some of Ren's research that would get him into a doctoral program or a biopharmaceutical company with his discovery of certain plants attacking specific cancer cells. Dr. Wellington took his findings, put his name on them, and was going to publish them."

Dr. Knight put his head in his hands.

Mari continued, "And Ren confronted Dr. Wellington. He said he just wanted to scare him. But Dr. Wellington taunted him and made him false promises. Ren became angry and lashed out, stabbing him and pushing him off the balcony."

"Oh, no!" Nichelle cried.

"Then I found the flash drive while weeding around the Clock Tower. I told Heather before I told the police, and Ren overheard. That's why he took Nepeta and threatened me—with a weeding scythe. He just lost it, thinking I would steal the research now. Joe and Heather came in just in time, or I might not be here," she finished darkly. Heather patted her leg, and Joe threw his arm around her.

"You've been through a terrible experience, Mari. But, you'll be all right," Dr. Fuller assured her.

"Thank you for exonerating me," Dr. Knight added.

"All right, let's work on getting back to normal and this program back on track," Dr. Fuller stated. "Please update me on your progress with your garden designs, changes, plants, by midnight tomorrow. Continue to work on the project and we'll discuss next week. Dr. Knight and I will be in our offices if you need us. And with that, we will wish you a good night."

After the professors left, everyone wanted to talk at once, but Mari was weary and didn't want to answer questions. Someone sent out for pizza. Mari wasn't hungry. She wanted to be in the room with Nepeta and finally let the tears come.

Heather whispered to her, "Tomorrow, let's go to the pub. Maybe Joe, Boothby, and the professors can come. What do you think?"

"Yes, Ma'am," Mari laughed.

The next evening, they gathered at the pub's large corner table, Heather, Joe, Boothby, Dr. Knight, and Mari. Dr. Fuller had declined the invitation. Dr. Knight brought Boothby, who complained that he seldom got into moving vehicles anymore and was happy with that choice.

When they received their drinks, Dr. Knight raised his glass of cider to make a toast, "To the end of this crazy debacle and the memory of Dr. Wellington. We may not have been friends, but seeing him go like this was sad.

"Life's going to seem pretty quiet without the murder drama," Heather commented.

"I'm sure we'll keep you busy when we get the program back in full swing," Dr. Knight said. "We have several projects to keep you busy – working in the garden and preparing for our next guest."

"Not another pompous professor," Joe groaned.

"No, no," Dr. Knight insisted. "You'll like this one. He's a textile artist, Will Dye. Also, we're planning a trip. Each session, we visit gardens somewhere in the world with the graduate students." He paused, and his eyes twinkled. This session's trip is to the UK, to Scotland to be exact."

Mari's eyes flew to Dr. Knight's.

"Yes, Mari, quite close to your grandparents. We'll be heading there next spring."

"Hurrah! That's fantastic!" Mari blurted out.

"Now, Boothby," Heather asked, "I'm sure you have great Meadowood stories over the years. Are you willing to share some of them?"

"Buy me another drink, and I'll be happy to entertain you," Boothby answered.

They laughed and Boothby settled into a tale of Meadowood fifty years ago.

THE END

ABOUT THE AUTHORS

James Brubaker is a voracious reader-turned-writer. He has a strong interest in sci-fi and fantasy. James enjoys integrating minute details, developing characters, and assisting with the plot in the Meadowood Garden mysteries. He co-chaired the successful Cecil-Con Convention, which celebrated all things sci-fi, fantasy, literature, gaming, and more.

For *Sharon Brubaker*, writing is like breathing. It's in her hard wiring. She is the author of mysteries, historical romance, romantic suspense, and spicy speculative fiction. She is a nationally award-winning author and educator. She is also an avid gardener, jewelry artisan, and artist.

Sharon & James are a mother and son writing duo.

www.MeadowoodGardens.com
www.Sharon-Brubaker.com

Instagram.com/AuthorSharonBrubaker

Facebook.com/SharonBrubakerAuthor

Tiktok.com/@AuthorSharonBrubaker